W9-AAK-348

scarlett dedd

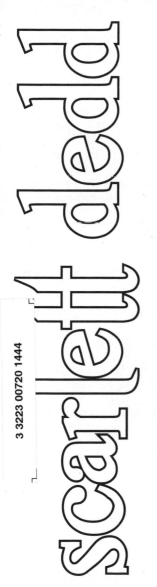

scarlett dedd

3 3223 00720 1444

READING
PUBLIC LIBRARY

INSTITUTED 1763

READING, PENNA.

CATHY BRETT

YA
Fiction
Brett

DELACORTE PRESS

This is a work of fiction. Names, characters, places, and incidents either are the product of the author's imagination or are used fictitiously. Any resemblance to actual persons, living or dead, events, or locales is entirely coincidental.

Text and jacket art copyright © 2010 by Cathy Brett

All rights reserved. Published in the United States by Delacorte Press, an imprint of Random House Children's Books, a division of Random House, Inc., New York. Originally published in paperback in Great Britain by Headline Publishing Group, a division of Hachette UK Company, London, in 2010.

Delacorte Press is a registered trademark and the colophon is a trademark of Random House, Inc.

Visit us on the Web!
randomhouse.com/teens

Educators and librarians, for a variety of teaching tools, visit us at
randomhouse.com/teachers

Library of Congress Cataloging-in-Publication Data
Brett, Cathy.
Scarlett Dedd / Cathy Brett. — 1st U.S. ed.
p. cm.
Summary: When misfit goth girl Scarlett accidentally kills herself and her family, she at first is amused by being a ghost, but then she begins to get lonely and bored.
ISBN 978-0-385-74175-0 (hardcover) — ISBN 978-0-375-99022-9 (glb)
[1. Ghosts—Fiction. 2. Blogs—Fiction. 3. England—Fiction. 4. Humorous stories.]
I. Title.
PZ7.B7555Sc 2012
[Fic]—dc23
2011022093

Printed in the United States of America

10 9 8 7 6 5 4 3 2 1

First U.S. Edition

Random House Children's Books supports the
First Amendment and celebrates the right to read.

Huge thanks, as ever, to N, M & D.

I am dead and there's nothing I can do about it.

I'm also mortified. I looked it up and 'mortified' is definitely the perfect word. It can mean two different things, both of which are me right now. Not only am I dead (which is bad enough), but I died because I made a stupid mistake. Stupid, stupid! And I killed my whole family. Urgh! HOW EMBARRASSING!

OK, I'm going to admit a guilty secret – I'd sometimes thought about my own death. I even imagined what my funeral might be like. You know, mourners in cool, black clothing, clustering around glowing shrines, hundreds of tiny candles flickering in jam jars, their dancing flames reflected in mounds of cellophane-wrapped flowers... A strangely-poetic mist swirling around their feet as my schoolmates file past my grave, each clutching a single, blood-red rose, which they drop on to my polished, ebony coffin, until it disappears under a massive pile of floral tributes, the cloying perfume filling the air with the scent of teen tragedy... My favourite band playing a rock track (specially composed for the occasion), the music pounding through the sobbing crowd... Tears pouring down pale, melancholic faces. As you can see, I had decided it would be atmospheric, extremely poignant, a little Gothic and, of course, very, very sad.

Huh! Yeah, right! Get real! Here's a pic of how my funeral actually looked –

– very, very damp!

Now that I really am dead, dead and buried, 'You're dead, Scarlett!' isn't a joke anymore. I wonder if all those brainless bullies – the ones who thought they were being SO clever – if they now feel kinda crummy?

'Scarlett, are you dead?'

How original! They never got it – never realised that I was inoculated against dumb phrases like that at a very young age. Even a four-year-old could see the potential for black humour in my name. Yeah, yeah, OK, very funny. It's just a name. Yes, I'm Dedd, Scarlett Dedd.

My dad, Wolfgang Dedd, never appreciated the suffering his name would cause to his kids. 'It's a strong, powerful, full-stop of a name,' he said once, 'perfect for a poet or a writer of literary fiction.' Well, that's fine for my dad, who is a writer (sort of), but not cool for me and my brother, Milton. It's been the source of endless juvenile ridicule. Cheers, Dad!

It doesn't help that my family are a bit… odd. In fact, when we were alive, we were notorious for our oddness. The oddest thing about the Dedds – odder than our name, our house or our unusual fashion sense – was our paleness. We were extremely pale. No, pale is too mild a word for our lack of colour. Our skin was translucent, blue-white – a sickening pallor, like bloodless corpses that just got delivered to the morgue in zipped-up body bags. How ironic! Our sad, watery eyes were the shade of doomed, ship-wrecking icebergs rimmed with bruise-like shadows. All four of us had this sort of limp, ash-coloured hair that had a sickly, mucus tint in summer, then dulled to the miserable hue of wet concrete in winter. Let's be honest. We were so colourless that we looked dead even before the accident.

Wait, I'll upload a pic...

See?

What I had never anticipated about my own death, even after long hours of dark, funereal daydreams, was all the vomit. I'd never imagined vomit. Not once. Who would? Death for me and my family was an extremely messy business and it was all my fault. I'm SO annoyed. Aaarrgh! How could I have been so stupid?

1

Scarlett the Zombie

Scarlett was miserable. She was miserable to be back at school after being miserable all summer. She'd spent most of the holidays in her room, pouting and frowning. Her whole life was miserable… and so unfair!

Being the eldest child of the oddest family in the street was no fun at all. Like watching a festering blackhead become an inevitable pimple, she'd just recently experienced the horrible realisation that nobody actually gets to choose their parents (or younger brother) and that none of us can mix up our own DNA recipe, selecting the best traits and dumping the weird bits. We just have to put up with what we get. Like pimples. Washing ten times a day and avoiding chocolate makes no difference. Scarlett was a Dedd. She would always have her mum's flat hair and tone-deafness, her dad's wide feet and cackling laugh, and the Dedd family sunshine phobia. Without buckets of cash for fake tan and hair dye, she'd be weird-looking forever. It was inevitable.

What she didn't have to inherit, she decided, was all the eccentric, organic-gardening, scrap-paper-hoarding, junk-recycling, tuneless-singing, spooky-smiling, head-in-the-clouds, loony-tunes stuff. She didn't have to grow up to be a total freak and it definitely wasn't her destiny to live a life without some luxury.

Her family might be misfits, Scarlett thought, and they might lack the funds for an endless supply of consumer goods, but why did all their clothes have to be second-hand? Which, by the way, doesn't mean gorgeous, vintage couture second-hand, but weird, Dedd-style second-hand, that no one else on the planet would want to wear. And why did their house (which wasn't even *their* house) have to be full of rejected and recycled furniture – damaged chairs found in a skip and sofas that tilted and stabbed you in the bum with their springs? Even the food they ate was *different*. Scarlett cringed at the grotesque meals that appeared nightly on their kitchen table.

Her dad tended a muddy plot in the garden in which he grew what he claimed were edible plants. These assorted, knobbly, olive-green, slimy objects (they were always olive green and slimy, not tasty and fresh looking, like vegetables in the supermarket) would be full of mud and oozing creatures and, once washed and de-loused, would lurk on the side of their plates pretending to be steamed Chinese cabbage or wild rocket salad.

Scarlett's mum would return from the weekly shop with hard, mouldy bread, like bags of floor tiles. Everything would be plastered in an acne rash of red sale stickers, having been selected during a rummage through the jumble of food on the 'bargain shelf'; there were apples with brown spots, potatoes sprouting tails, packets of broken biscuits and curled-edge, rubber cheese slices. Humiliating! The supermarket might as well have put up a big sign that said, 'FOOD FOR PATHETICALLY POOR PEOPLE'.

Scarlett wished with all her feeble strength that her family could be a little less odd and a lot more normal. One day, she pleaded, her dearest wish would be granted. She'd find the coolest outfit her friends had ever seen hidden on the rails in a charity shop. One day, Dad would sell his great novel or Mum would create an animated kids' TV series and they'd be able to buy a small car or bigger TV. One day they'd eat a meal that wasn't accompanied by green mush or garden slime. One day she'd go to school and nobody would make a Scarlett Dedd joke.

School! Oh no! It was nearly October and an event Scarlett had been dreading was looming like a giant, evil, flesh-dissolving poison cloud on the horizon. Her stomach flipped over at the thought of it. She'd barely endured the first days back after the summer holidays, when everyone had compared their tans and holiday pics. Scarlett didn't tan and the Dedds never went on holiday so she had prepared herself for the usual dumb comments, like how she must have spent the summer in a cave or a forest, wearing factor 500 sunscreen.

She'd got through it somehow (seeing her friend, Psycho, each day helped) but was now suffering another bout of gut-clenching, anticipatory trauma. There was far worse to come. In less than a week, her history class would be setting off on the Great War Trip – seven days in the WWI trenches of Northern France and six nights in a damp youth hostel. She couldn't face it. Feeling sick on the coach, then using communal bathrooms and having to get dressed with a load of other girls in a shared dormitory. Her baggy, grey underwear just wasn't up to it.

Not even Scarlett's friends (her slightly arty, horror-film-obsessed, video-making friends) could convince her it would be a fun experience, not to be missed.

'Isn't it su-perb? A whole week away from the 'rents,' Taz had suggested, sitting beside Scarlett at their favourite canteen table. 'And your idiot brother.'

'Hardly see them anyway,' Scar had replied, miserably.

'We can make a gory war movie,' said JP, stabbing his half-eaten burger. 'Authentic location an' all that.'

'Yeah, Scarlett, you could play a nurse amputating limbs,' said Ripley, with a sickening, manic grin. 'We should pack that scary rubber arm JP made for his zombie costume.'

'You could sit next to Psycho on the coach,' Taz whispered, but not quietly enough. Psycho, who was sitting across the table, poking at the melted cheese on his jacket potato, had overheard and his face flushed crimson. Scarlett was just about to say that she always got sick on coaches, when Psycho coughed.

'I'm n-not going,' he stuttered, then explained. 'C-county Swimming Trials coming up and a killing training schedule. Can't miss a session.'

It was yet another reason Scarlett didn't want to go. She sighed. More misery.

JP, Ripley, Taz and Psycho had become Scarlett's closest friends the previous year, much to her delight, after she'd played the part of a very convincing zombie in their amateur epic, *Zombie Saturday Checkout Girl*. The video got a thousand hits in its first week on YouTube and they'd been surprised to find that, not only was she perfect casting (Scar's look being a horror-film maker's dream), she was actually quite cool, too. AND, they were thrilled to discover, what Scarlett didn't know about classic horror movies and fake blood recipes wasn't worth knowing.

JP

RIPLEY

Taz

Psycho

Unaware that he had just reinforced Scarlett's determination to get out of the trip, Psycho picked up his lunch tray and shuffled across the canteen. On his way out the door, he glanced back at Scarlett from beneath his long, black fringe. Scarlett was still watching and he blushed with embarrassment again. Psycho was cute – at least Scar thought he was. Not cute like boy-band cute or fat-baby cute or fluffy-kitten cute, but the way his forehead creased up and his oversized ears wiggled when he talked and how his dyed-black hair grew blond at the roots... Well, he was sort of Goth cute. Maybe, if he was on his own, Scarlett thought, he wouldn't be so shy and she would actually have a chance to get to know him... accidentally bump into him at the horror comic store... sit next to him on the bus home and compare lists of Top Five Fave Blood-spurting Movie Moments.

She'd already attempted to get out of the Trench Trip by suggesting they couldn't afford it, but Dad had come up with the cash as soon as he heard it could be important for Scar's history coursework. She'd have to try something else. She'd break her own leg or pretend to be really sick – a brain-tumour sized headache or a rasping, consumptive cough. Or maybe she could have a gut-scouring, intestine-twisting stomach ache. But, whatever she tried, she'd have to do some pretty impressive acting to convince her parents because they weren't easily fooled. Perhaps she could become *really* ill, then she wouldn't have to act. What she needed was something that would give her an *authentic* stomach ache.

JP

Jake Pepper

... entered the "TOP FIVE Things
miss if they weren't there" test

1 football/Butts FC
2 mum's gravy
3 my glasses
4 'Warlock Frenzy III'
   - best fantasy game ever
5 Rip

"One Thing You Wouldn't Miss"
broccoli

Yesterday at 19.28
Comment...

send

SCREAMERS VIDEO CLUB MEMBERSHIP CARD

Jake Pepper
Membership Number:
00029
Fave Classic Horror Movie:
'American Werewolf in London'

funniest corpses ever!

What words best describe JP?
curly-haired – techi-nerd

SCREAMERS VIDEO CLUB MEMBERSHIP CARD

Anastazia Pinch
Membership Number:
00032
Fave Classic Horror Movie:
'Beetlejuice'

Taz hates her
name and plans to change
it 'officially' to Taz Legend
as soon as she's old enough

PILOT, PROTESTOR OR PRINCESS
Can a personality test
predict your future path?

Mostly Cs
PRINCESS
You are SPOILT! Probably an
only child, you have been given
everything you've ever wanted
by your doting parents since the
day you were born. As a result,
you are a bit of a pain and think
you're something special. Still,
your perfect teeth, those ballet
lessons and your unquenchable
self-confidence might land you a
job on the telly...
presenting the weather.

What three words best describe Taz? *talent – contest – wannabe*

13

My 10 Year Plan
by Rip

take back red boots
    and get refund
get rid of spots
win election ✷
study harder
pass exams
get into 1st choice uni
get top job
make lots of money
be happy

← send 🗑 →

SCREAMERS VIDEO CLUB MEMBERSHIP CARD

Ripley Muchmore
Membership Number:
00030
Fave Classic Horror Movie:
'Alien' **obviously**

RIP named after the character in the 'Alien' movies.

What three words best describe Rip? *ordinary – ambitious – deluded*

Psycho

SCREAMERS VIDEO CLUB MEMBERSHIP CARD

Tom Flint
Membership Number:
00031
Fave Classic Horror Movie:
'The Shining'

GOLD

BEST DIRETER

PSYCO FLINT ROOLZ

#2 Blood-spurting
Faves List - gushing lift

What ~~three~~ four words best describe Psycho?
part-Goth-part-fish

Toxic Risotto

Scarlett discovered the small, golden-yellow mushrooms in the park, near the swings, under the old climbing tree with the branches that hung down. She knew that mushrooms could be a bit tricky. Some were delicious and tasty, while others were psycho-deadly. Scarlett picked a handful and discreetly dropped them into her bag. She'd check out which they were, tasty or deadly, by doing a quick online search in the school library.

She couldn't get to the library until the end of the day and it was almost time for everyone to be chucked out. All the computers were being used by junior maggots, chatting online to their maggot friends or playing dumb fantasy games, which was really annoying, so Scarlett wandered into the Nature & Environment section and ran her fingers along the spines of the books. *The Hedgerow Larder* caught her eye because there was a drawing of a mushroom on the cover. She found a desk nearby and tipped her mushrooms out. They'd been slightly battered by the books in the bottom of her rucksack and tumbled on to the desk like musty, yellow punctuation marks; a question mark, a dash, a couple of exclamation marks: three commas and four full stops. Scarlett opened *The Hedgerow Larder* and found a page entitled: 'Identifying Fungi'. There was a picture that sort of resembled her mushrooms – right colour, right shape – and the caption indicated they MAY CAUSE MILD STOMACH UPSETS

Result! Here was the perfect way to avoid six nights of grey-teen-bra-exposure hell. She slammed the book with satisfaction, rammed the mushrooms back into her bag and went to look for another book – a book that would explain how to make something with the mushrooms that wasn't olive green, slimy or tasteless.

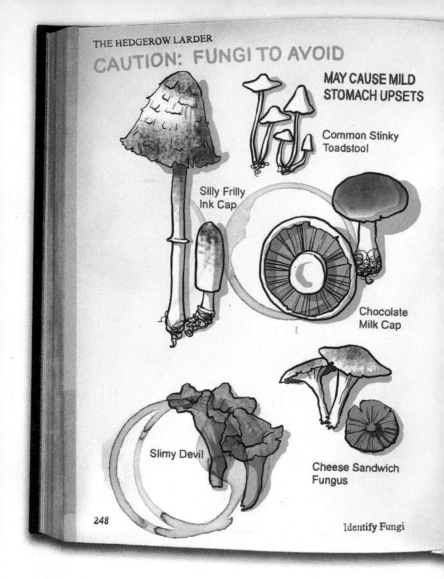

THE HEDGEROW LARDER

CAUTION: FUNGI TO AVOID

MAY CAUSE MILD STOMACH UPSETS

Common Stinky Toadstool

Silly Frilly Ink Cap

Chocolate Milk Cap

Slimy Devil

Cheese Sandwich Fungus

248

Identify Fungi

On Saturday morning, Scarlett found that she had the kitchen entirely to herself. She'd brought two books home with her, having dashed to check them out of the library before it closed, and now she opened *The Hedgerow Larder* again to confirm that her mushrooms did indeed resemble those pictured. What she

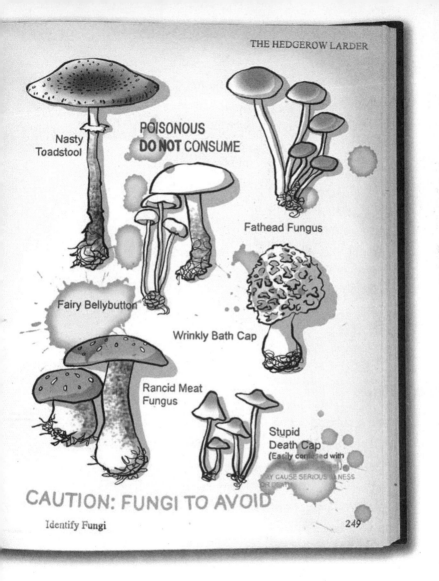

Nasty
Toadstool

POISONOUS
DO NOT CONSUME

Fathead Fungus

Fairy Bellybutton

Wrinkly Bath Cap

Rancid Meat
Fungus

Stupid
Death Cap
(Easily confused with

MAY CAUSE SERIOUS ILLNESS
OR DEATH

CAUTION: FUNGI TO AVOID

Identify Fungi

249

didn't do was bother to look at the next page. If she had, this story would have taken a completely different turn. It was the moment that Scarlett's fate was sealed. Of all the times in her life to be bored or distracted, this would have the worst consequences. Tragically, catastrophically, her mind wandered. She day-dreamed.

She began to paint a picture in her mind of bright lights and TV cameras and her older self having her hair spritzed and make-up dabbed, before launching into a slick, prime-time telly demonstration of the art of wild mushroom gastronomy. She sighed and smiled, deeply immersed in her fantasy, and failed to cast her eyes just a few centimetres over, on to the facing page entitled, POISONOUS DO NOT CONSUME where she might have spotted the photograph of an almost identical mushroom.

She reached for the second library book, a cookbook, and ran her finger down the index, looking for Wild Mushroom Risotto. Scarlett had decided that a risotto would be easy to prepare. She couldn't just eat the mushrooms raw (that would be disgusting, like eating compost, or something) and it would be fun to have a go at cooking. How hard could it be?

A small onion, she read.

A damp, wrinkled onion, with a tiny spike of green shooting out of the top, lay in the deep tray at the bottom of the fridge.

A large knob of butter

Risotto rice (Arborio or Carnavoli) – A handful of rice per person

There was a huge bag of rice in the cupboard and the other ingredients shouldn't be hard to find.

A glass of white wine (optional), she read.

Scarlett knew there were two bottles of wine upstairs in her dad's study. Two very expensive bottles that he was currently using as bookends while he waited for a special occasion (the elusive book deal) on which to drink them. But neither of them was open and neither was white. They would both be missed.

Hot stock – about one litre

This ingredient was baffling. What on earth was hot stock? The recipe suggested chicken or vegetable. Was it a kind of soup? They didn't have any of that. Perhaps she could mix brown sauce with some hot water. Good enough.

The last ingredient was the hard, Italian cheese that smelled of feet. This one was easy. Wolfgang Dedd kept his own stash of smelly-feet cheese in the larder. He was addicted to it. His habit was to grate it over everything, especially his favourite economy fish fingers, which tasted of cardboard and probably were cardboard, dunked in a fish tank for flavour. He'd buy a hunk of cheese, the size of half a car tyre, whenever he sold a batch of poems to a greeting-card company – appropriate, as they were pretty cheesy! He'd keep it wrapped in paper on a shelf in the larder, regularly hacking pieces off it, until it gradually disappeared. Then he would wait for another cheque to arrive so he could make the trip to the Italian deli to purchase the next one. It was one of Dad's rituals.

Scarlett could hear her dad engaged in another one of his rituals right then, as she chopped the onion. He was shuffling about in the room above, his study, a thumping pop song playing on his portable radio. It was his 'getting started' ritual. He always switched on a rubbish pop station when he couldn't think what to write. He'd listen to one, maybe two tracks and jiggle about a bit. He called it dancing. Supreme embarrassment! Dad said it was to get his ideas flowing. Amandine, Scarlett's mum, suggested that a spot of yoga or jogging or a brisk walk in the park would be more inspiring than jumping about to a boy band in his dusty study. But Dad liked the ritual. He said it felt like he *had* done a brisk walk in the park and he didn't have to change out of his pyjamas.

Scarlett pushed the chopped onion into a little pile on the board with the knife. She put a large, deep pan on the gas burner, then pushed and turned a button. There was a hiss of gas, then a click, click and a whoomp. A blue halo shimmered under the pan. Scarlett unwrapped the butter and looked at the recipe again.

A large knob of butter

She glanced at the kitchen door knob and back at the brick of butter, which she then cut in two, dropping one half into the pan. It sizzled and began to melt into a thick slick. Next she scraped the onions in. They began to bubble and spit.

A handful of rice per person, she read. Scarlett looked at her hands. That couldn't be right. A handful would be hardly any rice at all. Perhaps the book was written by a man – a big, fat, Italian man with huge hands. Scarlett looked at the front cover. Juliet Windsor. A woman and probably not huge or Italian with a name like that. She picked up the bag of rice and tipped a pearly mountain of the white grains into the butter.

Add one or two ladles of the hot stock...
Scarlett had forgotten the stock. She'd meant to look for the squeezy bottle of brown sauce and flick the switch on the kettle right at the beginning, but she'd been distracted by her dad's dancing. This cooking lark was more complicated than she thought.

The brown sauce was in the fridge but the bottle was almost empty with a congealed black scum around the lid. Yuck! She shook and squeezed and shook and squeezed until a dollop dropped into the large, glass measuring jug. The kettle clicked off sooner than she'd expected and, when Scarlett started to pour, there was a lot of steam but only a trickle of hot water. She had to refill it and switch it on again. The rice mixture in the pan crackled and began to smell like a bonfire, so Scarlett took it off the gas. It was all going a bit wrong. She frowned and pouted. The muddy, brown sludge in the measuring jug smelled lovely, though. Scarlett breathed it in. Maybe it wouldn't be a disaster. The rice might even taste better with those black specks in it.

Something hit the kitchen window with an alarming thump that made Scarlett drop the wooden spoon. Her brother, Milton, appeared briefly in the glass and ducked down. He resurfaced moments later clutching a football, grinned at her through the grubby window pane, then stuck out his tongue and made a rude hand gesture.

BANG

Scarlett blew a raspberry at him as he disappeared down the long garden path and through the undergrowth.

'Pttthhh! Stinking, maggoty monkey-boy!' she shouted.

The house had a very big garden which seemed to be endless, stretching back for miles and miles behind Dad's vegetable patch. Or perhaps it seemed endless because it was so overgrown. There were high brick walls on three sides, but you couldn't see the walls because bushes and twining climbers had long ago covered every millimetre. Actually, it was Scarlett's uncle's garden. Scarlett's uncle's house. Scarlett, her mum, dad and brother had moved into Uncle Oswald's house when they'd been unable to afford the rent on their own and when Oswald had suddenly disappeared. More of that story later.

Milton loved the garden; it was his domain. Some days it was his tropical jungle, full of poisonous snakes and deadly, man-eating spiders, on others, an alien spaceship, crawling with killer cyborgs and oozing, mutant space worms. He had built a den under a tree by dragging old doors and discarded furniture from the basement, and painted a sign that read,

⚠ WARNING
☠ NO adults
NO gerls
NO glita

The sign was the result of an incident the previous summer, when Scarlett had been determined to have a Hollywood, red-carpet, celebrity cocktail party in the garden. Milton had been horrified when his sister had arrived unannounced in his sanctuary, carrying assorted pots of glitter eye shadow, a string of feathered fairy lights, a net-curtain ball dress, sequinned gloves and a long, pink wig (all second-hand, natch). Scarlett had discarded the sequins and her fluffy, pink, girly phase forever a few weeks later. Her taste for shallow celebs and eye-popping glitz had dissolved overnight after watching a late-night horror season on E4, then discovering her uncle's horror poster collection, starring in *Zombie Saturday Checkout Girl*, becoming slasher-movie obsessed and painting her bedroom black. But Milton made the sign anyway.

Scarlett stirred the brown mess in the pan. It didn't look quite the way she had expected. She checked the book again. When should she add the mushrooms, she wondered? They looked a little bit muddy but she scooped them up and dropped them straight into the pan.

In a horror movie, this would be the moment when the scary, wooo-wooo suspense music would begin to get louder – scratchy violins and heartbeat drums.

Scarlett added the cheese then placed the pan on the kitchen table.

Screech, screech! Thump, thump!

It didn't quite look like the picture in the Italian cookbook but she grabbed a fork and tasted it.

Violins in a frenzy.

The risotto was yummy, a bit gritty (perhaps she should have wiped the mushrooms) and slightly bitter. But delicious. She was so proud of herself. She tried another forkful and another.

String section in meltdown and the drummer is having a massive coronary.

There was loads left in the pan.

Loud, pounding crescendo!

Then silence.

Long... scary... pause.

It hadn't worked. Scarlett felt fine. There was no sign of a stomach ache. She pressed the front of her jumper and felt the bump in her middle, where the mushrooms were now lying lethargically in her stomach. How long would she have to wait, she wondered? Had she eaten enough? She decided to go and lie down on the sofa in the living room for a while.

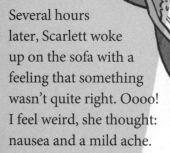

Several hours later, Scarlett woke up on the sofa with a feeling that something wasn't quite right. Oooo! I feel weird, she thought: nausea and a mild ache.

No, wait. It was more than an ache and worse than nausea. Much worse!

More hysterical violins!

She sprinted quickly out of the living room and managed to reach the threshold of the downstairs bathroom before a gallon of puke exploded from her mouth and nose, all over the walls and floor. This is unpleasant, she thought, very unpleasant, but definitely authentic. She lifted the lid of the toilet and chucked up again.

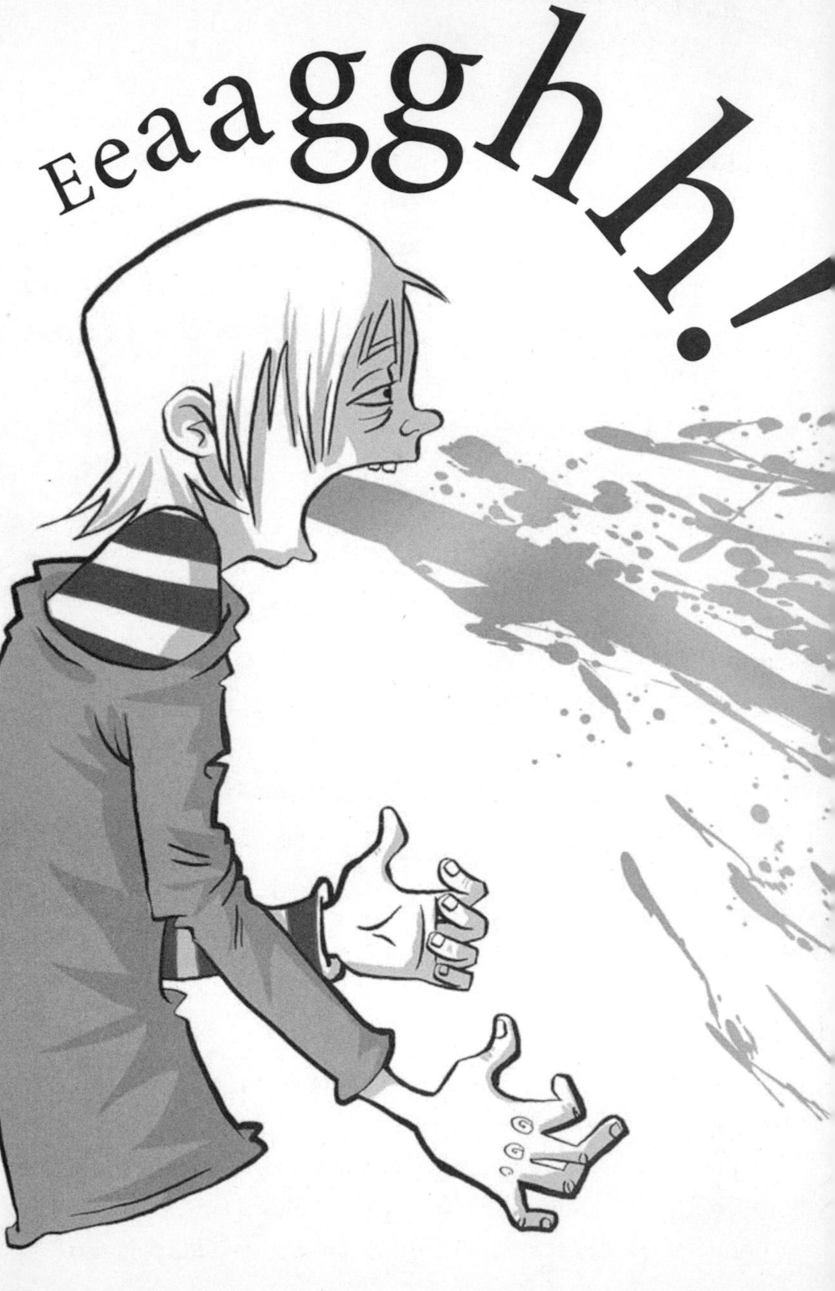
Eeaagghh!

Amandine Dedd was humming a tune in her illustrator's studio next door. Scarlett could hear her in the quiet moments between hurling and heaving. It wasn't really a studio, just an old, wooden, lean-to conservatory, but Scarlett's mum had moved out all the plant benches and seed trays and furnished it with a second-hand desk, an old hospital trolley for her paints and inks, and a tatty velvet chaise longue on which she dozed for most of the day. Amandine would waft around the studio or lie on the chaise, listening to a very old portable music-player (second-hand) at full volume. Scarlett's mum was French – born in the suburbs of Paris. That's not to suggest that her Frenchness was a reason for her wafting or lying on a chaise longue, of course. In fact, apart from her name, Amandine now felt she was more English than French. She'd lived away from Paris for so many years and spoke with a sort of funky French-English accent that men found cute and sexy. At least that's what Scarlett's dad would say on the rare occasions when he'd had a little too much cheap wine to drink. He would wave his glass, leer and pretend to grope Mum. Ick!

Scarlett, now in a contorted squat, halfway down the toilet u-bend, listened to her mum singing tunelessly. Even if Scarlett had called out, she knew that her mum wouldn't hear anything with her earphones in.

Heeuuuwww! You stupid, fat-headed moron, Scarlett, she told herself. What were you thinking?

Eeaagghh! Toxic mushroom risotto – big mistake!

BIG MISTAKE!

Scarlett's heart was just about to stop pumping, when Amandine, Wolfgang and Milton Dedd tucked into the cold leftovers for supper.

'This is great,' said Wolfgang. 'What sort of mushrooms are these?'

'A dunno,' said Amandine. 'A didn't make eet. A thought you deed.'

'No, not me,' said Dad, speaking with his mouth full and spitting a mushy glob of rice across the table.

'Scarlett made it,' said Milton, shovelling his spoon in and out of his mouth, like a grave digger filling a hole.

'She deed?' said Mum.

'Where is Scarlett?' Dad asked.

'Must be doing her 'omwerk … or chatting in a chatty room with her online friends.'

'Mmm,' Dad agreed, swallowing another mouthful.

Orchestra at blood-curdling, screeching full volume!

3

Multi-pack,
Buy-One-Get-One-Free
Funeral

Scarlett's friends were on the Trench Trip when, back home, the news broke of the Dedds' demise. By the day of their return, the quiet city suburb, a grid of tightly-packed houses around Sunshine Street, was buzzing with gruesome gossip of the quadruple poisoning tragedy and how the decomposing bodies hadn't been discovered for almost a week; not until a postman noticed a terrible smell.

Ripley, JP and Taz, who'd been sitting together on the coach home, were surprised to see their friend Psycho and their parents waiting for them outside the school. They'd planned to avoid their parents for a while by dragging their cases around the corner to the chip shop for some 'real food', before taking the bus a few stops, then finally walking home together across the park. The coach rattled to a halt, the brakes hissed and the exhaust belched blue, asthma-inducing smoke. The exit door swung open and the tired and dishevelled Trench Trippers began to disgorge and search for their luggage.

Psycho and the morose adults huddled together on the pavement, like conspirators.

'Look, they've got pictures of your house in this one,' whispered Taz's mum, holding open the middle pages of that morning's newspaper. JP's mother looked over her shoulder and peered at the story. It was yet another article about her neighbours, the Dedds. Taz's mum had started a scrapbook.

Psycho stared down at his shoes.

'I know,' said JP's mum. 'That ambulance and the police car were blocking the road all morning. Apparently it was a disgusting mess inside, you know. Took three days to hose the place down.'

'Eeewww!' exclaimed Taz's mum. She'd left her office straight after lunch so she could console her daughter but was starting to regret it. It was one thing having an excuse to bunk off work and catch up on all the latest poisoning gossip, but telling her daughter that her friend was dead… someone else would have to break the news to her, she decided.

Psycho sniffed, pulled his hood down a little further to cover his face then mumbled, 'Hadn't you better put that newspaper away?'

Ripley's dad coughed in agreement. He'd been trying to pretend he hadn't also bought that edition *and* cut out the article.

'D'you think they'll get a day off for the funeral?' said JP's mum.

Taz's mum tucked the paper under her arm as she noticed the teenagers were wandering towards them. The conspirators separated in a futile attempt at casualness.

'Funeral… what funeral?' JP asked his mum as he approached, yawning and scratching vigorously at his armpit.

'Jake, stop that!' said Mum. 'Didn't you wash today?'

'Didn't wash all week. It was great!' JP chuckled.

'What you all doin' out in the street?' Ripley asked, frowning. Her dad worked at home but he'd never come to collect her from school or a trip before. He knew she hated to be treated like a kid and she would always insist on making her own travel arrangements.

'I came home early because of...' Taz's mum started, scrutinising her fingernails.

'Yeah, we thought we should tell you...' said JP's mum.

Ripley's dad coughed nervously again. 'What she means is something's happened that...' He stopped and scratched nervously at his ear.

'You're all useless, worm-eaten, pus-headed wusses!' screamed Psycho... inside his head.

'Scarlett's DEAD!' gasped Taz, staring at the newspaper. She'd spotted the headline just visible under her mum's elbow and grabbed it from her.

'Yeah, we know – dead Scarlett, Scarlett Dedd, ha ha ha! Old joke,' said JP, sleepily.

'Oh... my... God! Shut up!' said Ripley, snatching the paper. 'She's not kidding. Look! Her whole family were *poisoned*! She's really dead!'

'Is that why she missed the trip and didn't return my messages?' asked Taz.

JP glanced at Psycho, looking for confirmation.

Psycho nodded and sighed.

The parents sighed too, with relief. They'd been spared.

'Wow! Cool!' said JP. 'No... I mean, that really sucks!'

'I miss Scarlett,' said Ripley.

'Do you?' Taz asked, pleasantly surprised. Ripley didn't seem to have found a way to express her grief yet, so Taz was relieved that she might, at last, be about to get her feelings out in the open. Taz stroked Rip's arm and smiled encouragingly.

'Yeah, she was the only actress we had that didn't need make-up.'

Taz pouted. 'Rip, you oozing plague-spot! Don't you care that she's dead?'

'Course she does,' said JP. 'She just doesn't feel the need to cry for five days and attend traumatised-teen therapy sessions.' JP always defended Rip, even when she *was* being an oozing plague-spot. He thought it was one of the requirements of being her boyfriend, like telling her she didn't look fat and letting her have the last chocolate biscuit in the packet. 'Anyway, we could ask that pale kid we saw today. The one who's so skinny, he looks like a vampire's sucked eight pints out of him.'

'He can't act,' said Rip.

'You mean he won't act, because he now hates you,' said Psycho. He was hunched under his black hoodie again, watching his archive of Scarlett footage on his video camera and trying not to think about how depressed he was.

'Yeah,' said Taz. 'Because you stuck a note to his back at the funeral that said, "Low Fat Option".'

'You saw that? Cool wasn't it?' said Rip.

JP and Rip high-fived.

'I definitely saw a tear in his eye,' said JP. 'We could use that in a vid somewhere.'

Ripley giggled. 'He's a pustule.'

'Well, he might actually have been upset about Scarlett,' suggested Psycho, sadly. 'Quite a lot of people are.'

'Mmm… s'pose so,' Rip conceded.

Ripley, JP, Taz and Psycho were sitting on a bench in the park, *their bench*, which was just close enough to the newsagent and chip shop for supplies of refined carbs and saturated fats, but surrounded by trees and therefore out of CCTV range. The bench was their after-school HQ, a place where they could moan about phoneys and losers, trash the teachers and plan their next gore-fest video project. They were still wearing their funeral clothes.

'Upset?' said JP. 'You know, sometimes, Psycho mate, you can be such a feeble, wet, slime stain.'

'S'cos he fancied her,' said Rip.

'Did not,' said Psycho, a little too forcefully to be convincing.

'S'not like you were married to her or something,' said JP, starting to chuckle. 'Scarlett the freak. Scarlett Dedd, the un-dead. Scarlett the zombie. Is this your ear that fell off, Scarlett?'

'Ooh, Scar, you're so pale,' sang Rip. 'What's that putrid smell? Is it Scarlett decomposing?'

'Stop it!' Taz shouted. She had just texted 'UR pox scab' to Ripley, even though they were sitting next to each other on the bench.

'Scarlett the vampire,' said JP, putting his hand over Taz's face and pushing her off the bench. 'You missed registration, Scarlett. Did you get out of your coffin late this morning?'

'Don't!' said Psycho.

'He doesn't mean it, Psych,' said Taz picking herself off the ground. 'Jay, you shouldn't joke about her like that. I know you're sad, too, and, you know, it's like they said at my support group, all that cruel stuff is just your way of coping, but you

shouldn't. Especially as...
I mean it's all true now, innit?'

'Scarlett the
ghost... whooooooo!
Watch out, or she'll
come back to haunt
us!'

...ut his head off!' JP yelled.

'I'm trying,' Ripley whined, 'but it won't. If you're so clever, why don't you do it?' she said, turning to JP and waving a pair of bloody scissors. A spray of red droplets leaped towards him across the path and spattered a crimson gash on JP's trainer.

'Hey! Watch it!'

Ripley scowled and sighed then turned back to the slumped, white body and her gruesome task. 'Why don't I just cut bits off?' she suggested. 'You know, like an ear or his nose or something.'

'Too Tarantino. Try using both hands and hack at his neck. You'll cut through if you keep chopping.' JP dragged his trainer through the grass and the blood smeared across the toe. 'Tssk. My new trainers. That's gonna stain,' he mumbled.

'You could always give him a layered fringe instead,' said Taz from behind a gravestone, where she'd been sitting quietly, picking bobbles off her jumper. Both girls sniggered.

'OK, Psycho, are you filming?' said JP, ignoring their laughter.

Psycho nodded. 'Yeah.'

'Mark it!' said JP.

Taz leaped to her feet, still chuckling, and picked up the home-made clapperboard which had been propped against a stone angel. '*Cuddly Bunny Meets the Hair Salon Slasher*, act one, scene one, take two,' she chanted in a bored monotone.

They all flinched as the gunshot crack of the clapperboard reverberated around the graveyard.

'Action.'

Again, the scissors flashed through the air and slammed, with a sickening thud, into the limp, white corpse. This time her aim was true and the force sufficient.

The neck was severed in a single **powerful** blow causing the startled head of the toy rabbit to tumble on to the *path in* a shower of red gore.

'Cut!'

.ter, the friends reviewed the footage.

'We'll have to film it again,' said Psycho.

'Can't you do something digital?' JP asked.

'Not really. It's there in all the frames, like a green mist or something.'

'There's something wrong with your camera,' said Ripley. 'You should take it back. Get a refund.' She picked up the tiny video camera. Cables dangled from it like curling entrails attached to Psycho's computer. The plot of their latest comedy horror video, *Cuddly Bunny Meets the Hair Salon Slasher*, consisted of a sequence of very gory 'haircuts' with a cast of horribly mutilated toys with limbs and eyes missing, or scissors and combs sticking out of their heads. They had left their location, the graveyard, as soon as the autumn sun had set and the temperature had dropped, then retreated to Psycho's house – a house with all-day central heating, a posh coffee machine and a handy supply of microwave pizzas and chocolate biscuits.

'It's not the camera,' said Psycho grabbing it from Rip and putting it back on the desk.

Rip sneezed and

dragged her hand under her nose, leaving a smear of snot. 'Eergh. I'm definitely sick, you know. Got flu or pneumonia probably.'

'Yeah, me too,' said Taz, feeling her own forehead for signs of fever.

'You're not ill. Anyway, if you are, you didn't get it off me,' said Rip, slumping down next to JP on Psycho's bed. 'You shouldn't have sat on that stone slab all day. No wonder your bum is so big and squishy.'

'Scarlett's grave,' said JP.

'What?' said Rip.

'Scar's grave. She was sittin' on Scar's grave all day.' JP stifled a smirk.

'...wasn't, was I?' said Taz with a shiver. 'Ooo, that's really spooky.'

'It wasn't Scarlett's grave. She's over the other side, you rot-brain,' said Psycho. He knew because he'd visited the four pathetic-looking mounds of earth and faded flowers earlier in the day, before the others had arrived at the graveyard. 'She doesn't have a stone slab, just a...' His explanation trailed off. They weren't listening.

'Don't give me your putrid diseases, will you?' said JP to Ripley, moving away from her. 'I've got footie try-outs next week. Got to be a hundred and ten per cent.'

'Rot off then, wart-features,' she replied, retreating to the other end of the bed. 'Just don't expect a snog later.'

'It's quite creepy isn't it?' said Taz, leaning forward over Psycho's shoulder and looking at the swirling cloud on his computer screen.

'What, snogging JP?' said Psycho. 'Yeah, creeps me out. Eergh.'

'No, that.' She laughed and pointed at the smudge on the video. 'D'you think it's a ghost?'

'S'not a ghost,' said JP. 'Was something Psycho did wrong – pulled out the cable or put his finger over the lens. Dung-brain! All I know is now we've got to mix up another batch of fake blood and put Cuddly Bunny back together again.'

4
Halloween Horror

Almost a fortnight before Halloween, late in the afternoon, JP was lying on his bed texting something rude but very funny to Ripley, when his mum's car alarm went off. Downstairs, JP's mum started screaming that she was on the phone.

'Get off your lazy arse, Jake, and sort it out!' she yelled.

JP put on his glasses and glanced out of his bedroom window but couldn't see any joyrider kids trying the door handles or anything, so he jumped down the stairs and grabbed the car's remote off the hall table. He knew his mum would give him an earful over dinner if he didn't do what she'd said and what he didn't need right now was an earful from Mum. She was finishing a big freelance job for a glossy PR firm and she was completely stressed out. When Mum was like this, he decided, it was pretty much like sharing the house with a bad-tempered, irrational, psychotic, eight-headed, ranting alien, and the last thing you want to do to a ranting alien is piss it off.

Out in the front garden, he clicked the remote button to mute the alarm, then reset it. The wailing continued.

It wasn't just his mum's car. All the alarms had been triggered, right down the street, and a trail of flashing amber lights flicked along its length in the autumn gloom.

47

That's when he saw the yellow kid's bike, with its wheel spinning, right at the end, outside Scarlett's house. He was almost certain that, when he'd walked out into the garden, the bike had been rolling past him. He'd seen it pedalling by out of the corner of his eye, but he couldn't have done because there was no rider standing beside it, nobody walking away from it. In fact, there was no one in the street. No kids playing, no adults trudging home from work. Nobody. People were only just starting to press their noses against their windows to see if their cars had been vandalised. One or two front doors were opening. The bike couldn't have been travelling along the road when he came out because the person riding it wouldn't have had time to get off it, throw it on the ground and run into a house. It was impossible. He'd have seen them.

Then a pile of leaves next to the bike exploded as if someone had kicked through them, and moments later, he heard the sound of a key rattling and a door slam. JP jumped like he'd just stuck his fingers in an electric socket. The door that slammed was the front door of Scarlett's house.

By Saturday night, JP had something extraordinary to share with the others.

'I'm not telling you yet. It's a surprise,' he said.

'So, why did we have to dress up and come to your house?' asked Psycho. 'Halloween's not 'til next week.' He was wearing a black cape, white face paint and fangs.

'I know, but I thought we could celebrate early,' said JP who had a knife through his head and wore a blood-splattered t-shirt.

'If it's that DVD of *Night of the Cheerleader Bloodbath* from your cousin,' said Taz, 'then you could have brought it over to Psycho's house, so we could watch it on the plasma.'

'It's not a DVD,' said JP, adjusting his fake knife.

'Awwww,' complained Ripley, who wore an all-in-one fluorescent skeleton suit. 'I was looking forward to watching that. My brother said it's brilliant; like, blood and brains spraying everywhere and there's a scene where a cheerleader is forced to eat her own intestines.'

'Eeuww!' said Taz, pulling at the bloody, rubber entrails that were tumbling out of the front of her t-shirt.

'Is it *Attack of the Werewolf Hamster*?' Psycho asked.

'Oh, I bet you got *Cannibal Drive-through Diner*, right?' said Ripley.

'It's not a movie, OK?'

'So what are we doing then?'

They usually went to Psycho's house because Psycho had an enormous fridge, loads of cool gadgets and a monster home-cinema system. JP hardly ever invited them over to the small, terraced, Victorian cottage he shared with his mum.

'All right, if you all just shut up for a minute, I'll tell you. You've completely spoilt the surprise, anyway. We're not staying here. There's a brilliant place I've found to do Halloween this year.'

'Are we going to the Nuclear Mutant Survivors' Party at the youth centre then?' said Taz. 'I thought all the tickets were sold out.'

'No, it's not the Nuclear Mutant Survivors' Party.' He paused.

'Yeah, and that's next Saturday, anyway,' Rip explained.

'What about going to a real haunted house?' JP continued.

'A haunted house? What d'you mean?' said Rip laughing and dancing about in her skin-tight, figure-hugging costume. She thought she looked really great in it.

'I mean a *real* haunted house... with *real* ghosts... of *real* dead people!' JP paused again for maximum effect. 'Real DEDD people.' He opened his eyes wide for emphasis. It worked. His friends were stunned for a moment into open-mouthed silence.

'D'you mean Scarlett's house?' whispered Taz at last, breaking the tension.

'Ooooh! Yes, please,' said Rip with relish. Nothing, however scary, could freak her out. The creepier the better.

'Are you going to break in? That's illegal,' said Psycho. His dad was a lawyer, though not the type that defended criminals in court, and Psycho was always saying things were illegal, as if he knew what he was taking about. 'We might disturb evidence in a crime scene or leave fingerprints or something. You know, get arrested by the police for burglary and stuff.'

'Well, if you don't have the guts, I'm goin' on my own,' said JP.

'I've got plenty of guts,' said Taz, giggling nervously and pointing at her gruesome rubber stomach. 'But I'm not sure we...' Unlike her best friend, Ripley, who was up for anything, Taz was a bit of a wimp. Rip said Taz's parents kept her in bubble wrap and she'd never have any fun if she didn't ignore them, break out, rebel and go crazy. It's what teenagers are *supposed* to do, Rip had explained.

JP tucked
his hands into
his armpits,
flapped his
elbows and
started making
chicken noises.
  'We'll
all go,' said
Ripley, making
a unanimous
decision for
everyone and
putting her hand over
JP's mouth to shut him up.

As the four friends walked the short distance to Scarlett's house, JP enjoyed telling them about what he'd observed since the day of the car alarms. There was something strange going on in the Dedds' house, he announced. He'd seen other things that he couldn't explain, like Milton's skateboard flying across the garden and the windows fogging up, like someone was breathing on them. Things that demanded further investigation.

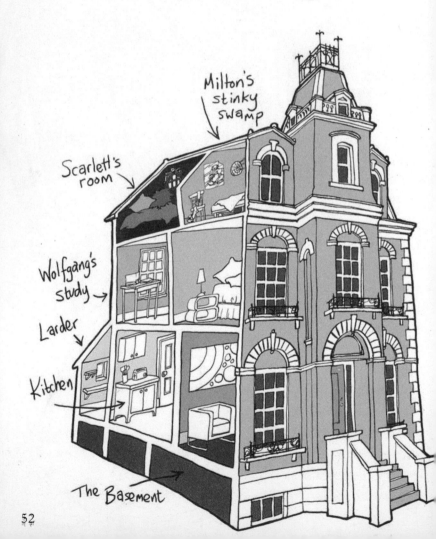

Milton's
stinky
swamp

Scarlett's
room

Wolfgang's
study

Larder

Kitchen

The Basement

He'd been watching the house for a couple of days; firstly from his own bedroom window, which gave him a clear view of the front, and then from the top of the climbing frame in the playground, behind the house. He'd seen other weird stuff from there, too, and filmed some of it with his phone. When he climbed up and shuffled to the opposite end to the slide, where the climbing frame was boxed in, and sat on the roof, he could see right over the garden wall and through the kitchen window. If he leaned forward a bit, now that most of the leaves had fallen off the trees, he could also see through one of the bedroom windows at the top of the house. The room had black and purple walls and he guessed that it must be Scarlett's room – definitely a Goth's bedroom. Scar never invited her friends over, either, so he'd never seen inside. He knew they lived there rent free and that it was her uncle's house, so they'd guessed that she was probably embarrassed about them not having much money, or something. JP regretted now that he'd never found a way to tell Scarlett that all that stuff didn't really matter. He wished he'd been able to persuade her to show him her vintage horror-film poster collection, too. It was probably awesome.

They reached the end of the street and stopped.

In the last few days, after school, JP was explaining, he had seen some very odd things indeed: magazines floating about, chairs pulling themselves out from under tables and then pushing themselves back in, a fringed scarf floating from room to room, and, strangest of all, a football slamming repeatedly against the garden wall. The annoying thing was that, when he'd played back the phone footage, it was a bit fuzzy and dark and shaky, with green tinted smudges, and it was hard to tell what he'd actually been filming. He'd decided he had to get closer. He needed Psycho's video camera and they had to get inside.

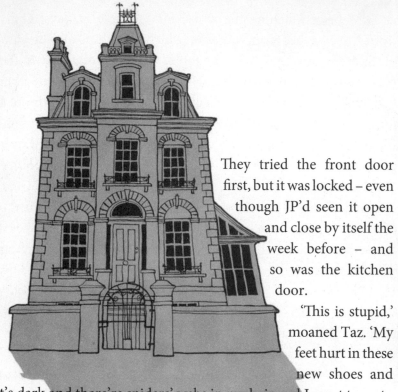

They tried the front door first, but it was locked – even though JP'd seen it open and close by itself the week before – and so was the kitchen door.

'This is stupid,' moaned Taz. 'My feet hurt in these new shoes and it's dark and there're spiders' webs in my hair and I want to go to Psycho's and watch a DVD.'

'Stop complaining, you walking liposuction accident,' said Rip, 'and look for a way in.'

The four circled around the house, pushing at windows and checking the strength of drainpipes, until they reached the conservatory. Psycho, who'd been too afraid to touch the house until now, in case he triggered an alarm, decided that it was a pointless exercise and they weren't going to find a way in, so reached aimlessly to jiggle the handle of the conservatory door. To his shock, the handle gave a hollow click and the door swung open. He whipped his hand away, as if it had been red hot, and covered his mouth to stifle a girly shriek.

'Shhhhh,' said JP, handing the torch to his friend. 'In you go.'

'Why me?' said Psycho.

'Go on,' said Rip. 'You scared?'

'No, just don't wanna get banged up for burglary. I won't get into uni.'

Rip pushed him through the door and they all watched, wide eyed, as he took a few hesitant paces into the darkness. He reached the far side of the room and the beam of the torch illuminated another door. He laughed, nervously.

'What's funny?' asked Taz and JP, who'd finally stepped inside.

'It can't be this easy,' he replied. 'Look.'

They gathered around the door in the evening gloom. There was a silver key sticking out of the lock.

'So, now what?' Taz whined. 'There's nothing here. Come on, let's go get some chips. I'm starving.'

They were now standing in the middle of the hallway.

'Shut up!' Ripley spat, ramming

her fist into Taz's upper arm. 'I thought I heard something.'

'Hey, you didn't have to punch me.' Taz's whimper echoed alarmingly in the empty hall.

'Shhhh!' JP hissed. 'There's someone moving upstairs.'

There was a faint rustling sound, like somebody was walking about wearing a cheap nylon tracksuit from the market.

'I've had enough of this,' said Psycho, with a catch in his voice. Being in Scarlett's house was making him feel really sad, so he was making a huge effort not to show it. 'It's not funny anymore, Jay. If something's going to jump out at us, we've guessed it's you. So, why don't you get on with it? Do your clever ghost effects or whatever, then we can go to the chippy, like Taz said.'

JP was climbing the stairs, hugging the wall, looking upwards, towards the first landing. He'd felt sick with apprehension since they'd entered the house. Now his heart was beating so hard that he thought it might leap out of his ribcage. He hoped he wouldn't throw up.

'Race you to the top,' yelled Rip, suddenly dashing past him. She sprinted up the stairs, two at a time, giggling as she went and stirring up a cloud of dust. As she reached the first floor, she grabbed the handrail, swung herself around with both hands and looked down at the others, out of breath.

'So, scare me then,' she shouted at JP.

'I… I'm not…' he began, then stopped, his face frozen in terror, as a glowing white shape loomed out of the darkness behind Ripley and floated above her head.

'Eeeeeeek!' Taz had seen it, too, and her scream ricocheted up the stairs.

Ripley whipped her head around, saw the shape and gasped. 'Aaahhh!'

The sound of their terrified howls punched through the house and reverberated down the length of Sunshine Street. Birds flapped from their roosts and children flinched in their beds. The white shape hung in the air then began a slow drift down the stairwell as the teenagers threw themselves across the hallway, grappled with the front door, wrenched it open, then slammed it behind them. *Bang!*

The draft wafted the white shape and sent it tumbling towards the floor, sailing in a sweeping spiral, until it skidded across the tiles and stopped.

5

Coma Vegetable

I saw this telly programme once about that post-traumatic-whatsit-doo-dah and one of the suggestions for coping with the stress and everything was to write it all down. I guess that's why I started this blog, so here goes.

Therapy Blog

From the beginning, how I found out I was... well, you know.

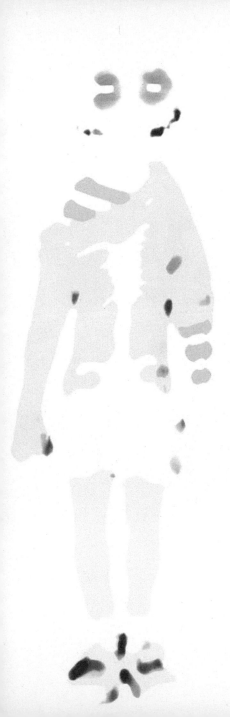

65

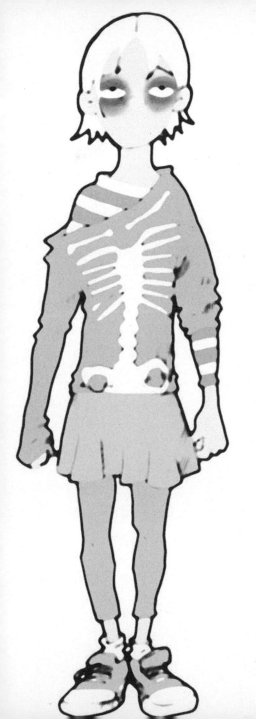

I woke up in the bathroom. Well, no, that's not completely accurate. I didn't exactly wake up in the bathroom; I found myself standing there, suddenly, in an instant, unable to recall what had happened the second before. I was a bit woosy, a bit wobbly, like when you stand on a cross-Channel ferry to France. The decks are solid but still sort of moving under your feet. Also, the white tiles on the walls seemed to be made of jelly – wobbly and heaving. Really freaky, right? I was standing in the downstairs bathroom (the same old bathroom in the same old house) but everything was completely different, completely weird and there was this funny smell.

In fact, although she wasn't aware of it, Scarlett had been in a sort of spooky semi-limbo in the days since she'd taken her last breath. First she'd been a musty, wet vapour, floating about at the morgue. She'd hung in the air above her actual body, oblivious to her own gory, entrail-prodding, CSI-style autopsy. Then she'd become a yellow dust cloud, like pollen, at the funeral directors' and, like pollen, she had made a number of people sneeze. Then she'd drifted about for a while at the cemetery as a pulsing, green mist. Now she was home again and about to discover that something really bizarre had happened.

Therapy Blog

I sniffed. What was that smell? It reminded me of pancakes. But why pancakes? Not the kind you have for breakfast, with syrup, but the pancakes my mum made sometimes, with... lemon juice. It was lemon. Lemon and something else. What was it? Bleach! I could smell bleach. Lemon and bleach.

The bath mat was missing, too, which was weird, because I was sure it had been there when I... when I... Oh!

Eergh! This disgusting picture popped into my head. I'd remembered the vomit... a lot of vomit! But it wasn't there now. Some extremely helpful person had scrubbed the bathroom with a yummy, lemon-scented cleaner. It must have been quite a yuck job to clear up all that mess and get rid of the revolting sicky smell.

I could hear my mum warbling in her studio and the occasional creak of floorboards above that confirmed my dad was still at his desk. There was even the faint sound of a football bashing against a wall in the garden. Phew! Everything was normal, I reassured myself. Then I felt another wobble coming on. Perhaps I'd been ill for a few days, like last January when I had that really disgusting flu that was going around, and I'd got out of bed too soon. But, I dunno, standing there in the bathroom, I didn't remember having been IN bed... never mind getting out of it. I decided to go upstairs and lie down for a bit. I'd feel better after a kip.

In the hallway, the black and white floor tiles were doing something strange. The checkerboard pattern seemed to ripple and surge with each step. I crept towards the stairs but never reached them, because I glanced in that fancy old mirror that's on the wall by the front door, and it stopped me in my tracks. It was a sight so shocking, so freaky, that I screamed.

'Aaarrgh!'

I'd expected to see what I ought to see, what you'd see, if you'd glanced in that mirror on your way across that hallway. I should have seen myself reflected there; my own pale, translucent face and hooded eyes, my own thin, grey hair and second-hand clothes. But the sight was of not myself... Nothing... Nobody. I wasn't there.

'I'm so ill, I've gone transparent!' I moaned. 'Oh, crap!'

Therapy Blog

Deep breath, Scarlett. Calm down and take a deep breath.

Writing that last post made me feel a bit panicky.

OK.

Next instalment...

Everything was a bit blurred, a bit fuzzy, and my transparent brain couldn't concentrate.

I needed to check something.

I wobbled into the kitchen to search for *The Hedgerow Larder*. The stupid book had promised me a stomach ache, not invisibility. I would make a complaint. I'd call one of those No-Win-No-Fee lawyers or something and sue the pants off the publishers. The book was on the table and the page was still open. There it was: **'may cause mild stomach upsets'.**

Right. That's what I thought. Stomach upsets. No mention of flu symptoms, gallons of puke or invisibility.

Wait a minute.

Something on the facing page grabbed my attention. Ha! Too blooming late to see that now, Scarlett! There was a picture of some almost identical mushrooms and beside them, the horrifying, sickening caption, partly obscured by a grease spot: 'Stupid Death Cap (Easily confused with Common Stinky Toadstool – see previous page). MAY CAUSE SERIOUS ILLNESS OR DEATH.'

Uurrrgghh! The book must be wrong. They can't have been poisonous. Deadly mushrooms, sitting there all innocent, in the park, where a little child could just pick them and die horribly... or a very stupid teenager, who can't read properly! Aarrgh!

I turned away from the book. I couldn't believe it! It was a dream. I told myself I'd wake up in a minute and discover I'd been in a mushroom coma or something. It was OK. I was actually lying in the semi-vegetable ward at the hospital and my family were sitting by my bed, deciding when to pull the plug on the machines keeping me alive and I'd start coming out of this really deep sleep and... Who am I kidding? I wasn't in a coma... I had to be mentally ill!

Angry with myself and the book, I tried to pick it up so I could throw it across the room, but I couldn't. Awwww! I didn't even have the strength to lift a stupid book. I was a pathetic, invisible, coma-vegetable, deranged lunatic! It was SO unfair!

Plunged into nauseating self-pity and depression, I went back out to the hallway. I felt so tired. It was as if the world was drifting in and out of focus and everything had become a million times heavier; exactly the way I'd felt after having that really disgusting flu. I should do what I'd wanted to do earlier:go and lie down. Perhaps a rest would make me visible and sane again, I thought. The staircase felt like the slopes of Everest, without oxygen. I managed to drag myself all the way up to my room on the second floor, then flop down, exhausted, on my bed.

I stared up at the poster above my head. A smiling skull leered at me.

'What are you laughing at, rot-face?' I hissed through gritted teeth. 'You should try being a deranged coma-victim sometime, or whatever. It's no picnic, I promise you!'

Depression had turned to fury. I rolled over, closed my eyes and rammed my angry fist into my pillow.

My fist kept going...

...through the pillow and, taking my arm then my body with it, went on through the mattress.

I sank through the bed frame.

My carpet.

Three wooden floors.

Copper water pipes.

More dusty carpets.

Ceramic floor tiles.

Right through the house and into the basement.

I landed with a bump.

Woah! That was a bit unexpected!

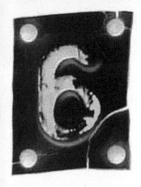

Grim Death

Therapy Blog

So, where was I last time? Oh, yeah. So, I fell through the floor. It's called Anger-fuelled Rapid Passage. LOL. Sounds like something you'd suffer after eating a bad curry! A.R.P. for short. But I didn't find that out until I'd endured hours of complete panic and confusion. It was a nightmare! I'm a bit embarrassed to admit that I went kinda loopy. Y'know: raving, loco, screwy, off my onion, bats in the attic. But, can you blame me? I was, like, *Stay calm, Scar! You're invisible and you sank through the house, but it might only be temporary. It doesn't necessarily mean you're, y'know, never gonna get back to normal again...*

...or that you're dead, or anything.

I started hyperventilating, then stupidly wondered if breathing was now completely pointless, because I might not actually *need* to breathe anymore, which made me feel even worse... so I kinda fainted.

When I'd recovered from my mini-meltdown, I had this genius idea. When I'd had the flu, Mum had gone online to check the symptoms weren't brain damage or Ebola or something. I could do the same and look up my mushroom-vomit, falling-through-floors thing.

Up in Dad's office, I opened the laptop, switched it on, waited for the connection, then typed in:

> mushroom vomit invisible sinking mental

I carefully tapped the return key and waited.

There's a lot of bizarre stuff out there in cyber-chat land. I guess you knew that already. But, if you go looking for answers, especially to really, really important questions like mine, don't expect to find them without wading through a load of freaky, scary weirdness! I suppose I should have expected a few odd results from my slightly unusual search criteria, but *please*... Welcome to Planet Demented, or what?!

I kept following links to wilderness survival sites or super-realistic, rubber, fake-dog-poo manufacturers. Then I found this kind of emo-teen chat room where there was a whole thread about poltergeists' skills, which looked more promising, and another link to this:

Ghost goss, corpse cringes, death disasters? Swap your sad cemetery stories here

scardeparted: i kinda sank thru my bed just now… is this normal?

2ghoul4skool: ooo… what did it feel like?

toxicboy: back-off U tourist! she's in shock… just UR bed? were U annoyed at the time?

scardeparted: actually i sank thru my whole house! v scary and yep, was a bit miffed!

toxicboy: ARP

Therapy Blog

Found out today I'm suffering from P.T.D.D. – Post Traumatic Death Disorder. Got the diagnosis from that website I found. Y'know, ghoolkool. Some kid in the chat room – same one who told me about A.R.P., I think – said it's going to take me a while to finally comprehend that, not only am I invisible, but I'm probably not alive any more. Mmmm. Need to think about that for a while. Later...

OK. After a hundred queries and online searches, I guess I'm finally going to admit the truth.

I'm dead.

I'm actually dead. Dead Scarlett Dedd. Oh... my... God! I'll need years of psychoanalysis.

What I had trouble trying to work out was this: if I'm dead but I'm still here, well almost here, does that mean I'm a ghost? It's completely freaking me out. And is this what a ghost is supposed to feel like – really, really strange with a dose of blind panic?

Ghoolkool has been very helpful, but I kinda wish first-timers, ghost-virgins like me, were provided with a guardian angel, or someone who could show me how being dead is done. Someone to hold my hand or make me a nice cup of tea. That would make it so much easier.

Therapy Blog

Now that I've calmed down about the dead thing – y'know, less loon and more semi-loopy – I've been thinking about sinking through the house. Like, if I could pass through floorboards and carpets and stuff by mistake, then perhaps I could do it on purpose. Y'know, maybe I have some of the abilities that ghosts are supposed to have; abilities like walking through walls. They always do that in movies, right? And making objects move and stuff. They're all kinda essential skills for persons of the apparitional persuasion. Sinking through the house and landing in the basement was sort of embarrassing, but it was a mistake, wasn't it? So it was probably the supernatural version of a toddler toppling over when it tries to walk. I wonder if I might have to learn how to ghost-walk and ghost-sleep and ghost-run and ghost-sit and ghost-carry things, like being a baby all over again. That'd be *really* frustrating!

It took a while for Scarlett to build up the courage to test her theory. The first thing she decided to try was putting her hand through her bedroom door. She took a deep breath and held out her right index finger, then pressed the door panel. The top of her finger disappeared.

'Oh!' she yelped, and staggered backwards with the shock. She looked at her finger. It was still there and appeared to be OK. She reached out again. This time with her whole hand. She closed her eyes and thrust her fist forward. She opened one eye.

'Hey, awesome!' she said, reaching out the other arm which also disappeared through the door, up to her elbow.

'Get out of here! That's so cool!'

It felt like dipping her hands into warm bathwater. It was great. Should she try her whole body? Scarlett screwed up her face, took a step forward and stumbled straight through the wall into her brother's room. She wrote in her blog:

'The sensation was strange but not unpleasant, like walking through long grass or wading in a swimming pool. The movies appear to have got it right. So far.'

Next, she spent a bit of time working out how to control the wobbling, falling and sinking. Sinking right through the house only happened when she was angry, according to her chat-room mates, but moving about in her new ghost-bod was a bit like walking on ice. Her interaction with floors and solid objects had changed somehow, so she had to balance and anticipate the direction of her body, then calculate the force required to propel herself in the other direction. It was tricky but she started to get the hang of it, even though it made her ghost-muscles ache.

She discovered, by accident, that she could float. She'd been doing the walking-through-walls thing again, pushing through from the kitchen to the hallway and back again. Some parts of the wall, where the layers of wallpaper were particularly thick, were harder to get through. On the fifth pass she caught her shoulder on the chunky moulding of a piece of Victorian anaglypta wallpaper. She fell forward, scrunched up her eyes, and waited for a stomach-churning lurch, but, instead of the unpleasant tingle of half-sinking into tiles and floorboards, she felt nothing, only a slight sensation of being horizontal rather than upright. When she opened her eyes, she was floating three metres above the hall, drifting up the stairs, like Superman. Hey! she thought. This is fan-stinkin'-tastic!

The realisation that she no longer had to go to school was another cause for celebration.

http://scardeparted.blogspot.com

Ghost Training Blog

Yay! I won't have to do another maths exam ever again. I will never be forced to wear my minging, second-hand, faded sports kit and run around the playground in freezing rain while pretending to play netball. I won't have to stand up and read Shakespeare's sonnets while people make faces or flick chewed, paper spit-balls at the back of my jumper. In fact, from now on, I can do whatever I want, can't I? I have an empty diary and nothing much else to do but try out my new ghost skills. I could practise all day if I want to. And I think I shall.

Excited by her new project, she did some floating again and worked on increasing her speed, finding that she didn't have to waft in a sedate fashion, but could dash about like an insect. She was still pretty clumsy though, often tumbling through walls by mistake or putting a flailing arm or leg through items of furniture. But her enthusiasm for speed-floating soon dwindled when her ghost-body started to feel like it was out of juice. She was exhausted and starting to wonder if she'd ever get it right. Thank goodness she didn't have to take an exam in it. It was all so much more difficult than she'd thought it would be. And, she concluded, she was hopeless at it.

Low ghost-esteem brought her training programme to a halt.

http://scardeparted.blogspot.com

Ghost Training Blog
Urgh! I guess I'll never be a ghost gold medallist. Not even
if I train for a hundred years.
In fact, I'm pretty rubbish.
I am a limp, useless, lifeless corpse!
I am an oozing lump of rancid bog-slime!
I am a waste of ghost-space!

Scarlett sat on the floor in her room and stared out of the window.
She sighed and her ghost-breath hit the window pane and fogged
the glass.

Woah!

Somehow, she was able to fog up the window as if she was
still alive! She blew again, harder, and this time her ghost-breath
turned to frost and spikes of ice crackled across the surface. Cool!
A brilliant new skill. She reached out to write her name in it and
got as far as 'Sca', before the tip of her finger disappeared through
the window and the ice melted.

Setting Off Alarms

Towards the end of her first ghost-week back in the house, Scarlett was starting to get the hang of it. If she took plenty of rest breaks, she could whoosh about and float through multiple surfaces with ease and she could feel her ghost-muscles getting stronger. She could lower the temperature in rooms, write messages on mirrors and windows, lift small objects and open and close doors. However, she hadn't yet considered why her family (who all appeared to be happily occupied at their respective tasks in the office, conservatory and garden) had not abandoned those tasks to mourn her demise. She had been too self-absorbed to wonder why her parents weren't expressing heart-rending grief at the loss of a daughter or why Milton wasn't fascinated with having a corpse for a sister. She'd not yet discovered that they were themselves as unaware of her death as they were of their own.

Scarlett stood in the hallway. She could hear Dad typing upstairs, Mum humming in the conservatory and the rumble of Milton's skateboard on the concrete path down the side of the house. What Scarlett needed now, she concluded, was a test of some sort. She had to try out her abilities. But how and what and where?

http://scardeparted.blogspot.com

Ghost Training Blog

Woopee! I have complete freedom to do whatever I want. Here's my plan:

1. I'll go to the cinema and watch all those gory horror movies I'm supposed to be too young to see. Nobody can stop me. Ha!

2. When a hottie pop star hunk or yummy Hollywood actor comes to the city, I'll walk through the walls of his luxury hotel and leave sexy messages on his bathroom mirror so that he'll become mysteriously obsessed with me and can't figure out why.

3. I will glide into the vaults of the Bank of England and, after rolling around in piles of banknotes for a bit (I've always wanted to do that), I will stuff billions of pounds into a couple of those big wheelie suitcases and give it away to the needy people of the world. This will include sick children in Africa, landslide victims in South America and that woman in Hampshire who rescues hedgehogs. Aww, they're so cute!

Being dead must have made Scarlett a bit stupid. You've probably worked it out already, but Scarlett took several minutes to realise that none of her plans would actually work. Of course, she would be able to walk *in* through the walls of the Bank of England, but she couldn't take suitcases with her and wouldn't be able to get the money *out* again. The money and the suitcases weren't invisible or able to pass through walls. Duh!

And, while it might be enormous fun to make a pop star hunk or Hollywood hottie infatuated with a ghost-girl, she and the hunk/hottie would never be able to date. Also, the hunk would probably get drug tested and checked into a mental hospital or rehab or something if he let slip that he had an 'invisible' girlfriend!

Finally, the whole point of getting in to a cinema to watch one of *those* movies, is so you can boast about how disgusting it was to your friends. Scarlett didn't have friends she could share stuff with anymore. They were alive; she was dead. She really missed them – even their teasing.

Scarlett glanced at her invisible non-self again in the mirror. What should she do? She was a ghost and had a unique opportunity to do *anything*. It was ridiculous that she couldn't come up with a plan. She looked around the hallway for inspiration and spotted last month's copy of *Book of Darkness* magazine – a very cool fanzine for Goth bands and indie horror movies. Her mum had put it on the bottom step of the stairs, which in mother language means, 'Take this rubbish up to your room or recycle it.' It was the issue that included an interview with the gorgeous Si Storm, her favourite rock star, and Scarlett had read it about a hundred times. She decided to nip down to the newsagent on the corner to see if the next edition had hit the shelves yet, then she'd spend the rest of the day in her room, reading, listening to Si's band and deciding what to do next.

She picked up the front-door key from the hall table.
She had worked out that, once she'd got the mag and brought it home, she would need to open the door to bring it inside. Out on the top step, she was confronted by a web of police tape, stretched across the entrance, that said,

POLICE / DO NOT CROSS / POLICE / DO NC

She giggled then wafted through it. The tape tingled as it cut her into **six pieces**, then she popped back into a whole again and stepped out into the bright autumn sunshine. She floated down the steps and looked out of the gate, down the length of the street.

There was nobody about. It was the time of day when people were just about to leave work but kids were already home from school and surfing the net, watching telly, or having baths. Mums were sticking ready-meals in the microwave or checking online auction sites to see how the bidding was going. The residents of Sunshine Street didn't notice the gate of Uncle Oswald's house creaking open and an invisible foot kicking a pile of brown leaves into the air. They didn't see the child's discarded, yellow bike lift itself off the pavement and pedal along to the Eight 'til Late newsagents where it leaned itself gently against a litter bin. Mr Kumar, the owner, failed to spot the edition of *Book of Darkness* that jumped off the shelf, hung in the air then danced out of the shop. Nobody but Scarlett ever bought the magazine and Mr Kumar supposed, since the 'incident', that he'd have to cancel the order from now on.

'Bye, Mr Kumar,' Scarlett shouted, as the door closed behind her. Mr Kumar ignored her and continued to read a newspaper advertisement for thermal socks. He wasn't really ignoring her. He'd simply not heard Scarlett's voice. She hadn't yet discovered that, to the living, her ghost-voice simply sounded like a badly tuned radio in another room or the rumble of far-off traffic.

On the way back, the child's bike zigzagged down the middle of the road. Scarlett was getting a bit frustrated that her impressive performance was going to waste. She'd have to do something more dramatic than shoplifting and bike riding. There was a red light blinking on the dashboard of JP's mum's car, at number eleven, which gave Scarlett an idea. As she passed it, she concentrated, stuck out her foot and kicked the bumper as hard as she could. The car juddered and the air was filled with the screech of a siren.

Wwweeeeeeaaawwweeeeeaaa!

She kicked again and, one after another, all the cars along Sunshine Street began to wail, their hazard warning lights flashing frantically. Scarlett grinned at the fanfare that accompanied her back to the front door of Uncle Oswald's house.

Uncle Oswald

This is a good moment to explain a little more about Scarlett's uncle Oswald and how the Dedds moved from their previous home and came to be ~~living~~ dead in his house in Sunshine Street.

Wolfgang Dedd's brother, Oswald, was a kind of local celebrity – for all the wrong reasons. According to the gossip, he was either a bank robber on the run, a cyber-criminal, a drug dealer or a terrorist. These wildly inaccurate rumours had started when, two years ago, he had suddenly disappeared. One day he was there, the next he was gone. Sunshine Street had positively fizzed with speculation. Was it improper behaviour or mass murder, perhaps, that had caused Oswald to flee? What *had* he done? Was there a juicy scandal? Or a nasty, dark secret?

In fact, it was none of the above. He'd fled the country (that much was true) but his reason for running was far more mundane… and rather embarrassing. The residents were quite disappointed when the truth was finally revealed. He'd been gambling in an online casino and, to finance his habit, had foolishly borrowed money, at a frightening rate of interest, from a notorious local gangster – a seriously scary bloke called Simon Bunting. Simon 'Liquidiser' Bunting. Not only did Oswald owe thousands to Bunting, but he'd found out, too late, that the casino website was owned by the very same scary gangster. 'Liquidiser' had issued spine-chilling threats, via his nasty henchmen, to 'fulfil payment obligations now or face the consequences'. Oswald did neither. He didn't have the ready cash and the 'consequences' were too terrifying and grisly to contemplate, so he simply ran away.

A few days after Oswald disappeared (to South America or Bulgaria some had guessed) a package arrived from the Dedds' cowardly relation. Scarlett's dad placed the package on the tiny breakfast table in their tiny kitchen in their tiny house, and the family gazed at it in thoughtful silence. They were all wondering what lurked inside the small, white, padded envelope, sent from Spain.

Milton hoped it was presents. Uncle Oswald was good at presents. Usually they were small, expensive, electrical things, so, naturally, Milton hoped it was small and electrical… and for him. Scarlett's guess was far more gruesome. Perhaps, she imagined, the package wasn't from Uncle Oswald at all, but from that big, fat cheat, Simon 'Liquidiser' Bunting, whose henchmen had taken Oswald hostage and were keeping him chained up in a warehouse somewhere.

Simon
Bunting

The package probably contained his severed left ear with a blood-splattered note from the henchmen wrapped around it saying,

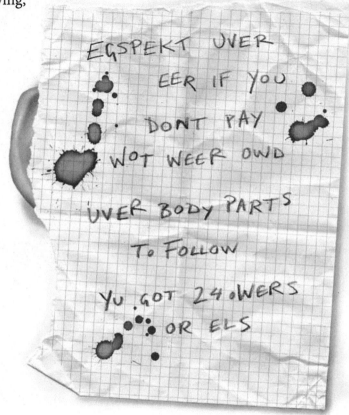

EGSPEKT UVER
EER IF YOU
DONT PAY
WOT WEER OWD
UVER BODY PARTS
To FOLLOW
YU GOT 24 oWERS
OR ELS

Mum was apprehensive, too. She suggested, quite illogically, that it might be a letter bomb and that Dad should take it out to the garden, place it carefully in a bucket and 'turn the 'ose on eet.'

Only Dad guessed correctly. He knew exactly what was inside. He ripped off the top of the envelope, while Amandine winced behind a box of cereal, and tipped the contents on to the table. A set of keys fell out with a loud clatter. Mum yelped then peered over the top of the Choc-Puffs box.

'Kiss? Why is
ee sendin' us kiss?'
she asked.

'I knew it,' said Dad. 'He wants us
to keep an eye on the house in Sunshine Street.'

Moving into Uncle Oswald's house in Sunshine Street came at just the right time for the Dedds, as they were very close to being turned out of their own. Although Scarlett's dad, Wolfgang, was the co-author of the trendy, cult graphic novel, *Pirate in Green Sneakers* (you may have read it if you're a bit 'arty', though probably not), he'd written almost nothing since. Nothing that was good, anyway. He hadn't sold an article or a short story for months. Their savings were dwindling and Amandine's infinitesimal income (earned painting bunny and superhero murals on playroom walls) wouldn't cover their rent for much longer. Minutes after the keys hit the kitchen table, they were on a bus to Sunshine Street.

Uncle Oswald's house was great. It was huge – at least
ten times the size of theirs. It stood, on its own, at the end of
Sunshine Street; a street of large, medium and small houses,
which were huddled together in a cosy, friendly way. Oswald's
house was different, sort of standoffish and aloof. There were
house-sized spaces on each side, as if it had stuck out its elbows
and nudged its neighbours out of the way. Behind the house was

a children's playground and behind that stretched the grassy expanse of Buttercup Hill. Beyond the hill you could see the rooftops, spires and oddly-shaped skyscrapers of the city. The Dedds opened the gate, walked up the steps and Dad turned the key in the front-door lock. They stepped inside and stood in the hall, gazing upwards.

'Let's explore,' said Dad.

There was a large living room with tall windows, a dining room, a kitchen and a bathroom off the hallway downstairs, then five bedrooms and two bathrooms on the two upper floors, and a sweeping staircase winding through the middle. Below was a cellar, with cupboards for storage and a sort of den/office/games room. In the den/office/games room there was a sofa, a full-size snooker table and a large safe, its door left wide open with a few bits of paper inside. There was very little furniture in the house, just a kitchen table, a couple of chairs, one bed, a few strange paintings and a collection of classic horror-movie posters. It was just as it had been the day Oswald escaped on the Eurostar. He'd even left a half-finished cup of tea and a cheese and pickle sandwich (now green and mouldy) on the kitchen table, confirming that he'd vacated the building in a hurry.

Scarlett found a cream envelope with 'Wolfgang Dedd' written on it, propped on the mantelpiece in the living room. She handed it to her dad. Inside was a hastily scribbled note in pencil:

Wolf,
House is yours.
Deeds in safe.
Tell everyone I'm dead.
Sorry, Oz

9

Sick

Scarlett's first adventure as a 'newbie' dead person had been fantastic fun… at first. She'd got a real buzz stealing the mag, kicking the cars, setting off all the alarms and zooming down the road to a chorus of wailing. Fantastic, until she began to feel sick. The street was stirring but so was Scarlett's stomach.

Oooh!

She didn't feel so good. Curiously, considering her new-found ability with walls, Scarlett had tripped over the curb and stumbled through a pile of leaves. She bounded across the pavement towards the house, her triumph turning, almost instantly, to misery, her smile to a grimace. When she'd staggered up the steps and then tried to lurch through the front door, the magazine still in her hand, she'd lurched straight back out again. *Book of Darkness* pinged out of her grasp. Although she knew it would delay her for several seconds, she picked up the mag then fumbled with the door key, breathing rapidly in an attempt to keep her stomach contents down. Once she'd got the door open, at last, and fallen inside, she slammed it with a kick of her foot and made a frantic dash for the toilet bowl. She wasn't going to make it.

Eeeuuuwwww!

A shower of vomit gushed over the floor of the hallway and Scarlett doubled over.

'Ohhhh, f-f-festering fudge!' she yelled and chucked up a second time, making a vast puddle of ghost-puke that stretched from the kitchen door to the bottom of the stairs.

'Eeeuuuwwww!'

Over and over, she retched and spewed until, quite empty, she lay on the stairs, too weak to lift her ghost-feet out of the ghost-mess. That was horrible, she thought.

I hope that doesn't happen again. Ever.

'Scarlett! Don't just lie in it,' said Dad, stepping over her slumped body as he came down the stairs.

'What?' Scarlett mumbled, a bubble of puke-snot popping from her nose.

'Get a bucket and mop it up now, before it starts to dry.'

Scarlett opened her eyes and watched her dad skirt around the evil-smelling puddle and walk *through the wall* into the kitchen.

'Dad!' she yelled, then closed her eyes again, not quite believing what she'd seen.

'Yes?' said Dad, popping his head through the wall again.

'You just walked through that wall,' she whimpered.

'Did I?' said Dad's floating head. 'Oh, yes. So I did.'

http://scardeparted.blogspot.com

Emergency Therapy Blog
DIS...ARSE...TER!!
MY FAMILY ATE THE 'SHROOMS!!

After Scarlett had hit the mouse button and posted her Emergency Therapy Blog, she dropped angrily through two floors and joined her dead family, now gathered in the kitchen. Calmed somewhat by the physical exertion of cleaning the hallway floor, but still incredulous, she asked about their lethal risotto meal.

It was suppertime and Mum stood by the open fridge, staring inside, wondering why Milton wasn't hungry. He was always hungry. Actually, now that she thought about it, she wasn't hungry either – hadn't been for several days. Perhaps she was still getting over her upset stomach, she thought.

Dad looked thoughtful for a moment then began to explain that he, Mum and Milton had, indeed, eaten her delicious risotto and, he conceded, had had a slight 'reaction'.

'But I feel all right now; quite recovered,' said Dad.

Milton was playing with the knobs on the front of the gas cooker and the room was beginning to fill with the unpleasant, slightly eggy, smell of gas.

'But you're not all right,' said Scarlett. She didn't know how to break it to them. 'The mushrooms…'

'Zay were awfully tasty,' said Mum. 'Well done, Scarlett, ma petite.'

'They were awfully something,' said Scar. She spotted the *Hedgerow* book on the table, still open at the same page. Genius! That's how she'd explain it. 'Look. Here.' She stabbed her finger through the criminally ambiguous illustrations.

'Mmm?' said Dad.

'Ooo, lovely pictures,' said Mum, stupidly. 'Who ees zee artiste?'

'I don't care about the stupid artist, Mum. Read the festerin' caption!'

'No need to be rude,' said Dad.

'Oh,' said Mum. She'd read it and the implication was beginning to sink in. She looked at Scarlett. 'Do you mean ZOSE are zee mushrooms you put een zee risotto?'

Scarlett nodded.

Dad was still reading. Then he also got the message and sat

down. 'That explains a lot. Ha! I thought I was going a bit ga-ga. Y'know, cuckoo, cuckoo!' He drew circles on his temple with his finger.

'Meelton. Do stop playing with zee cooker,' snapped Mum. 'You'll blow us up or gas us all to de... Oh!'

I'm FURIOUS! Not only am I a dead, traumatised teen-ghost but now I have ghost-parents and a ghost-brother, too. My whole annoying, freaky family have come with me to 'the other side'. And it's ALL MY FAULT! How could I have been so stupid? I only wanted to miss a school trip and ended up missing my WHOLE LIFE! Why did I make that stupid risotto, and why did I cook so much of it? Then, to make my ~~life~~ death even more intolerable (if that were possible), I've just had ANOTHER shock. I'm a ghost, right? But I have just cleared up a pool of my own ghost-sick. What's that all about?

Video Evidence of the Existence of Ghosts

'Psycho, it's starting,' Taz yelled up the stairs. 'Get down here. Bring the pizza.' She went back into Psycho's basement home-cinema room and joined Ripley, who was sitting on a sofa, hunched over a complicated remote control. There was the sound of feet running downstairs, then the door opened again and Psycho stumbled into the room, dropping the steaming cardboard pizza box that had been delivered onto the coffee table. He'd given the whole box a few seconds in the microwave and now it was volcanic-lava hot and searing the flesh off his hands.

'Is he on yet?'

'No,' Rip and Taz both replied. 'Not yet.'

On the giant TV, the title sequence was ending with a guitar riff, the rumble of drums and a female voice-over: 'Welcome to *Fakers*.' The shot switched to Ozzy Garlik, the presenter with the ego the size of a planet, who was sitting on the *Fakers*' famous purple sofa. Someone was sitting beside him, almost out of earshot.

'Jaaayyy!' screamed Rip, making Taz jump. 'It's him! Those are his jeans; that's his hair!'

The others agreed. It was definitely JP's leg they could see on the sofa next to Ozzy Garlik. Their friend was on the telly. At least his leg was.

'Should have been you, Psych,' said Taz. 'It's your video.'

'It's OK. I don't mind.'

Actually, Taz thought it should have been her that got to go on *Fakers*. After all, of the four of them, she was the most photogenic and the one who had the best chance of a telly career. She knew all the tricks about spotting which camera to look at and how to avoid touching the microphone pinned to your clothes or pull out the mass of cables tucked around the back.

'Shh,' said Ripley. 'I can't hear what he's saying.'

The camera had zoomed in slightly while Garlik was introducing the show and now they couldn't see JP's leg anymore. Ozzy Garlik was running through all the stories from the week's news, games and video host sites that he was going to prove to be lies, fakes and hoaxes.

'But first, we're gonna start our special Halloween show with a ghost story. Always a favourite at this time of year,' he said with a wink and an unpleasant smirk. 'Here's a video you might have clicked on this week. In fact, I'm almost certain that all of you did, 'cos it had more hits in twenty-four hours than almost any previous so-called ghost footage. Send your granny out the room, 'cos this one's seriously disturbing, dude!' Garlik looked to his right and a fuzzy, grainy image appeared on a plasma screen behind him. The

image cut to full frame and the video began to play. The title appeared, white on black:

Rip, Taz and Psycho had seen the footage before, of course, but they were mesmerised nevertheless. They'd edited it together a couple of days ago, in Psycho's bedroom, using Psycho's computer. It was Psycho's film but, as ever, Jake decided to put his name on it as director. It was the creepiest two-and-a-half minutes of video any of them had ever seen. Even the expensive

CGI stuff they did in Hollywood studios didn't compare with the scary footage Psycho had filmed on their second visit to Scarlett's house last Sunday night. It was mind blowing. Most of the 'ghosts and poltergeists in my house' type stuff on the net is really fake looking. You can tell it's been done in someone's kitchen with a load of fishing line (to pull chairs across the room) or in a university dorm in freshers' week, where someone has discovered the night-vision button on their new video camera. It's all really lame.

Their video was different – different because it was real.

The first image was of the outside of the house: a towering, creepy silhouette, lit from behind by the orange glow of the street lights. Then it cut to a door opening. The director of the TV show cut from the footage to the studio audience and Garlik for a reaction shot. They were hooked. The next bit was quite jiggly as Psycho, who was holding the camera, walked up the stairs after Jake, along the landing and into Wolfgang Dedd's study. Then it cut to a close-up of JP standing at the window, holding some pieces of paper. Again the director left the video and showed the faces of the studio audience. They'd lost interest and were beginning to look bored. Wait until they see the next bit, thought Ripley, grinning.

They stared at the screen. The video continued.

The next reaction shot showed the audience were also staring, some open-mouthed, some hiding behind their hands. Brilliant, thought the three friends. Just the reaction they wanted.

The climax and the last, amazing, sequence…

The video came to an end and they cut back to a medium two-shot of Ozzy Garlik and JP. Rip stifled another excited scream with the collar of her jumper. On screen, Garlik leaned back. His face was pale and his self-important smile had disappeared for a moment. Suddenly his face twitched back into its usual disdainful expression and he grinned menacingly at their friend. It was time for the interrogation. JP blinked at Ozzy behind his glasses.

'Wooooooo! Scary stuff. So, Jake Pepper. JP. Welcome to *Fakers*. You shot this infamous vid last weekend. First off, where's this weird-looking house?'

JP cleared his throat. 'It's a house in my street… where a friend of mine used to live.'

'Don't you mean, "where she still lives", 'cos she's a ghost, right?' said Garlik, mockingly.

'Yeah. That's right.'

'Your vid, it's very clever and spooky and all that, like everyone's saying, but it's bogus, innit? How did you do that last effect?'

'It's not bogus. It's Scarlett. It's what she did.'

'So, you actually expect us all to believe that this amateurish, home-made, digital fake is a real vid of the ghost of your dead girlfriend doing freaky things?' Garlik laughed.

JP looked briefly at the camera. He had to correct Garlik, because he knew Rip and Psycho would be watching. Rip was his girlfriend and Psycho was the one who fancied Scar. 'You don't have to believe me if you don't want to. But she's not my girlfriend and it's not a fake.'

Garlik laughed even harder, then looked at the studio audience for confirmation. 'Ha ha! I should hope not! If you had a dead girlfriend your parents would think you were crazy or, y'know, smokin' wacky-backy!'

JP scowled. His mum was in the hospitality suite next door (called the Green Room for some reason, even though the walls were beige) watching the interview. She'd definitely be regretting getting caught up in the whole going-on-TV excitement and eventually giving in to his incessant pleading to appear on the live show. JP looked at the arrogant presenter. 'I thought this interview was gonna be about Scarlett,' he said, 'and how we think she's trying to contact us… me and my friends… y'know, from the grave.' JP had come to the studio that day determined that he wasn't going to be ridiculed like other guests had been. But it was going wrong. Ozzy Garlik had thought Scar was his girlfriend and now he wasn't taking him seriously. Hadn't he watched the video? Hadn't he seen the strange, creepy stuff Scarlett had done? Hadn't he been listening to Jake's explanations?

'Your friends?' said Garlik 'You've got friends? OK, so, you think this dead girl is trying to tell you something?'

'Yeah,' said JP. 'We…'

'Something like, "Get a life, you losers!"'

The following evening, at Psycho's house again, JP's friends tried to cheer him up.

'It wasn't so bad,' said Ripley.

'Yeah, it was,' said JP, miserably.

'But you got to meet Ozzy Garlik,' said Taz. 'And go on telly. That's so cool!'

'Oh, woopeee!' said JP, with as much sarcasm as he could muster. He was totally humiliated.

'Forget it,' said Psycho again. 'It doesn't matter if they believe you or not. Fact is, we got more hits than almost any other video this week. We're famous. Think what we could do with our own stuff now. We should post *Cuddly Bunny* next.'

'He's right,' said Taz. 'We're celebs, aren't we? Doesn't matter what for.'

Taz's Haunted House Interview

JP's telly appearance did make them mini-celebs at their school. Psycho was asked for his autograph, which was an unexpected thrill, and Taz, desperate to make the most of her fifteen minutes of fame, agreed to a video interview with a spotty junior news reporter, for the school's website.

Here's a transcript:

INT. CLASSROOM, BUTTERCUP HILL SCHOOL – DAY TAZ and hyperactive reporter, 'DIZZY', sit on the desks, their feet on chairs, while Dizzy's mate, the CAMERAMAN, is cleaning the lens of an expensive, heavy video camera on a tripod – property of the school's media studio. Apart from the three of them, the classroom is empty. It's lunchtime. Dizzy taps the microphone he's holding and stands up. The cameraman, who's wearing headphones, raises his thumb and disappears out of shot, behind the camera.

DIZZY: (*to camera*) Interview with Anastasia Pinch for the *Buttercup Hill Gazette*. This is your school news editor, D-Zee Dizzy Dan Jackson, reporting. (*turning to Taz*) OK. So, Anastasia… do I call you Anastasia?

TAZ: It's Taz; just Taz.

DIZZY: Taz. Your mate Jake was on that *Fakers* show the other night, right?

TAZ: Yeah, but we all made the vid. We're a team and, like, all four of us work on all our movies. It's a collaboration.

DIZZY: (*quite impressed*) Yeah? Cool! (*waggles a thumbs-up gesture at the camera as if he's a cool dude or a rapper, which he obviously isn't*) Did you do stuff on that *Fluffy Bunny* vid, then? That was awesome! Really disgusting!

TAZ: *CUDDLY Bunny. Cuddly Bunny meets the Hair Salon Slasher*. I did all the make-up and effects on that. (*pause*) Well, some of the make-up… and Psycho designed the effects and my best friend Ripley made the bunny… but I helped. And I mixed up the syrup and food colouring for the fake blood.

DIZZY: (*less impressed but still squirming with excitement*) Eergh! Excellent!

TAZ: I act in them sometimes and I can sing and…

DIZZY: You have singing in your movies? Didn't know you made horror musicals.

TAZ: No, well we don't exactly. But that's what I want to do, y'know, when I leave school. I'm going to go to drama school to learn acting and dance… and then get discovered and make proper movies in Hollywood.

DIZZY: (*clearly not interested in Taz's movie-star ambitions, glances at the camera, makes a 'this is so tedious'* *face at his mate, then waves his microphone impatiently)* Can we get back to the video – the one in the house?

TAZ: Yeah. Course.

DIZZY: *(reading from his notes)* Um. I've got some questions. Right. That vid was really cool. How did you do it? Can you tell us how you did all those effects. How you made the…

TAZ: *(angry)* S'not effects! That's the whole point, you retard!

DIZZY: But, I thought...?

TAZ: It was all REAL. It's so STUPID that nobody believes us.

DIZZY: *(looks at his mate again and grimaces)* Hey! No need for hostility, babe. *(clearly annoyed the interview is going off track)* Tell us what happened, then. Go on.

Convince us you really did film a ghost.

TAZ: (*takes a deep breath*) OK. I'll tell you the whole story. (*looks directly into the camera*) We didn't know what to expect, me and my friends, when we went back to the haunted house that night, but we knew it would be scary. We never dreamed it would be so scary, so terrifying, that we'd never be able to wipe the horrific memory of it from our brains. Not in a million years of psychotherapy!

DIZZY: (*now mesmerised and leaning closer with his microphone*) Really?

TAZ: We had discovered a way to get inside the house when we went the first time. This door was left open, so we weren't breaking in or anything.

DIZZY: Why'd you run away the first time?

TAZ: Well, there was this piece of paper.

DIZZY: You were scared by a piece of paper?

TAZ: No. Yes, but we thought it was a… it doesn't matter. There were other things – noises and stuff. We thought we heard noises like people moving about. A person. Then this white shape kinda floated out of nowhere and tried to attack us. We thought it was a crazy serial killer hiding in the house or something and it was pretty creepy. You would have been scared, too.

DIZZY: (*grunts*)

TAZ: So when we saw it had just been a

piece of paper, we kinda relaxed. I said, 'There's no such thing as ghosts, right?' (*pause*) Little did we know how wrong I was. (*raises eyebrows, her eyes wide as saucers*) Then JP started to walk up the stairs.

DIZZY: So, you followed him?

TAZ: Yeah. (*beat*) There was a rustling noise, the same noise we heard before, and we wanted to find out what it was. JP and Rip went into this room where it was coming from and I kinda peered around the door. (*miming her actions*) I shone my torch inside and there they were, hundreds of pieces of paper, like, scattered all over the carpet and Jay was pointing at a window that was open at the bottom, just a crack. Me and Psycho stood outside. We didn't want to...

DIZZY: Too scared?

TAZ: No! Well, a bit... but Psycho was kinda freaked out. He said it was probably Scarlett's dad's office and we shouldn't touch his things. He said it was—

DIZZY: (*excited*) What? Like disturbing a grave? Ooh, d'ya think that was why she—?

TAZ: (*shocked at the thought*) No! I dunno. (*frowns*) You keep interrupting and putting me off.

DIZZY: Sorry.

TAZ: So... (*another deep breath*) Then JP was leaning over the desk and he picked up a pile of paper and began to read. (*mimicking*

JP's voice) 'Barnaby Bunny lived with his mummy bunny and daddy bunny in a pretty, little house on Sunshine Street. They were very happy little bunnies.' It was something like that. Then he says, 'This is rubbish!' I guessed it was something Scar's dad had written, so I said, 'Mmm. Not much of a loss to children's literature, was he?' We all laughed – except Psycho, actually, who said we shouldn't be mean and that his teddy-bear book was OK and that he really liked the pictures. But then Rip reminded him that Scarlett's mum did the pictures.

DIZZY: (*sighs*) When are you gonna get to the bit with the…

TAZ: Computer? Just getting to that. So, Psycho said, 'Hey, all this stuff is still switched on…

plugged in.' He opened the laptop on the desk and said, 'This model is really old – practically an antique.' The screen flickered and this box appeared where you have to enter a password. JP said he thought they would have cut off the electricity after the… you know. And I told him it was probably because it wasn't their house.

DIZZY: Belongs to their uncle or somebody, duznit?

TAZ: Yeah. And that was what Psycho was just starting to say when, whooooosh! (*mimes flapping object*) ...something fluttered over by the door and this thing flew past JP's ear and flapped across the room, like a demented paper bird. We all kinda yelled and I picked the 'bird' up off the floor. It was a copy of *Book of Darkness* magazine. As I stood up, another shape whistled past, missing the end of my nose by a millimetre. (*she makes a 'tiny' sign by pinching her thumb and forefinger*) I'm not exaggerating. I yelled, 'Stop chucking stuff!' The object landed on the desk and bounced into the wastepaper basket. It was a trainer, one of SCARLETT'S trainers! There was a sort of clicking noise coming from the desk and we all looked at the laptop. A line of dots was appearing in the password box. This kinda screensaver photo of Scarlett and her family filled the screen and they stared at us. That's when we started to get REALLY freaked. (*the camera zooms in slowly on Taz's face*) JP was saying, 'What did you do, Psych?' And Psycho said, 'I d-d-didn't touch it. How would I know what the password is?', The screen flicked again and the white box of a new text document appeared. Rip told JP he was awesome 'cos she thought he was doing it, like it was a Halloween trick. He's really great at special effects and stuff, so I guess she thought he was trying to scare us. But he said it wasn't him. There was another click… and another. This time we could see the keys dropping down as if an invisible finger was tapping out the letters. If it was a trick, I thought, it was pretty freakin' brilliant. With each tap there was, like, another letter… and it slowly spelled out, GET OUT OF MY HOUSE! (*the Zoom has reached extreme close-up on Taz's eyes and mouth.*) We froze. (*pause*) I wanted to run but it was as if my feet had been, like, glued to the floor. My heart was hammering and I couldn't believe what I was watching. It couldn't be real. It was a joke programme someone had left on the laptop or, y'know, it'd been set up to run when somebody opened it. (*reaches out, takes hold of Dizzy's arm and looks him in the eye*) Then the window thing happened. I saw the glass in one of the window panes – it was white, like when you breathe on it. Then the one next to it did the same. Someone was breathing on the glass, but they couldn't be because there was NOBODY THERE! Like, the whole window was breathed on and there was this kinda weird, lemony smell. Then an invisible finger began to write a message. (*writes in air with her own finger*) 'GOTCHA!!! U R SO EASY 2 SCARE LOL SCAR x' I took a step back and my cheek hit something hard.

It was a wooden chair… and it was floating above my head!

DIZZY: (*squirms*)

TAZ: You've got to believe me. We didn't do any of it on Psyche's computer and there were no wires or threads or anything. (*agitated*) Then IT happened. There was this really strange smell, then this whoosh of wind blew all the paper in the air and it sorta stuck.

DIZZY: Stuck? Stuck to what?

TAZ: I dunno. It just stuck to a… a body. The paper just became the shape of a person…

. . . and the PAPER PERSON
RAN OUT OF THE ROOM!

Consequences

Scarlett's haunting stunt hadn't gone exactly to plan. Nor had it had quite the effect she'd anticipated. She'd really enjoyed spooking them, more than almost anything she'd yet done as a ghost, but maybe she'd been a bit full on and scared them away forever. That would be a disaster. She didn't want to frighten her friends so much that she got rid of them. She wanted them to visit *more often*.

When her friends came back into the house that second time, the sick thing happened again. Just like the time with the bike. She thought she'd done a brilliant job; first, by chucking stuff, then with the messages on the computer and the window. But, as she'd tapped at the keyboard and dragged her ghost finger across the frosted glass, she'd felt a dreadfully familiar wave of nausea.

'Not again,' she moaned as, while holding the chair, the ghost-vomit rose from her gut and sprayed out of her nose. She was covered in it. Ghost-head to ghost-foot. When a huge draft from the window lifted all the sheets of paper into the air and they actually stuck to her, it was revolting. Eergh!

Another visit to Ghoolkool provided some answers.

Ghost goss, corpse cringes, death disasters? Swap your sad cemetery stories here

scardeparted:	why do i keep puking?
examy:	bulimia?
scardeparted:	duh! not on purpose!
dying4U:	U R reliving UR 'death experience'… happens sometimes
grimdD:	if U died by your own hand… even accidental
scardeparted:	how do i stop it?
toxicboy:	no contact
scardeparted:	with my friends?
toxicboy:	best avoided if U snuffed yourself
grimD:	bet U REALLY miss them…

Scarlett hovered at the kitchen table, opposite Wolfgang and Amandine, and scowled at them. She was in a big, fat, pouty ghost-mood. Why hadn't she made the connection the first time she projectile ghost-puked? Now she understood the horrible disadvantage of death by mushroom poisoning. Trying to make contact with her friends had consequences – unpleasant, vomity consequences. Being dead was going to be a very big pile of stinking, putrid, contaminated waste if she couldn't do a bit of simple haunting without getting pukey.

And her boring ghost-parents were now acting just like live-parents. They were stopping her from having any ghost-fun at all with her new abilities. They'd probably make her do ghost-chores instead, and they'd still tell her when to go to bed, what to wear, not to slouch, not to swear. It was going to be ghost-hell!

Why do rents think not slouching and cleaning your room are more important than anything else in the universe? Why do they think they know your friends better than you do? And why do they want to know every detail of where you've been, who you've been with and exactly what you've been doing with them? MIND YOUR OWN FESTERING GHOST-BUSINESS! Worst of all, why do parents tell you what it was like when they were teenagers? I mean, how irrelevant is that? Duh! Who cares that Mum used to walk twenty thousand miles to school every day, carrying a mountain of chemistry textbooks? Who's bothered that Dad had about a hundred part-time jobs when he was fourteen – in a coal mine, cleaning toilets in a prison, haddock fishing in the Arctic... or something like that? And when they say that they always did exactly what their parents told them to do, without question, no way do I believe them. NOT FOR A MOULDY-MOGGOTY-MICROBE-MINUTE!

'We just want you to be 'appy, Scarlett,' said Mum, resting her elbows on the kitchen table. They sank into the wood, so she placed her hands back in her lap.

'And we both think it's not a very good idea to scare your friends like that,' said Dad. 'You saw what happened.' He was standing by the window looking out into the garden.

'Eet is such messy every time. Disgusteeng,' said Mum, scrunching up her face.

'And thousands of people have seen that video they made, you know, Scar,' said Dad. 'What are we going to do if they all turn up here?'

'We're all finding eet 'ard to change for our new life… I mean death, aren't we?' said Amandine.

'Yeah, but…' Scarlett began.

'We've discussed it,' said Wolfgang. 'No contact with the living, OK?'

Scarlett's mum and dad had just finished explaining to her that they too had experienced the unpleasant consequences of making contact with the living. Wolfgang had, he said, written an email to his agent and had blown chunks all over his cardigan when he'd clicked 'send'. Amandine had picked up the phone, speed-dialled her friend Sabine, and spewed a sticky ghost-puddle all over the chaise longue. She'd had to lie in it all afternoon as she'd been too weak to move.

'Terrific,' Scarlett spat. 'So what d'you expect me to do all day, then? Sit in my room and knit?' She scowled and hunched her shoulders.

'Your brother has found lots of things to do,' said Dad, as he watched Milton swinging upside down from a tree branch, gouging a bogie out of his nose with his finger.

'Yeah, eating worms and farting,' Scarlett mumbled.

'You 'ave books and music and your fashion-design projects,' said Mum.

'Film projects,' Scarlett corrected. 'But, what's the point if I'm gonna be locked up in this stinking, lemon-scented, sweaty-armpit of a house by my boring 'rents for the rest of my… forever. It's so unfair!' She stomped across the kitchen, heading for the door. Or rather, she floated through the door in a stompy way. 'I wish I was dead!' she yelled, then, embarrassed at the stupidity of what she'd just said, returned to open then slam the door as hard as she could.

'No texting, Scar,' called Dad, as Scarlett shot up the stairs and into her room.

All the dreams I had when I was alive have to be screwed up, shredded and dumped in the recycling bin now that I'm dead. No more GCSE coursework or taking exams or going to uni or film school and becoming a creative director in Hollywood. I'll probably never get older than I am now or get to do adult stuff. I'll never get kissed – properly – or have sex with a boy or squeeze out a screaming baby – actually, prob a good thing! I'll never be asked out on a date by Psycho – I *know* he was gonna – or share secret stuff with Taz again or spot cream with Rip. Worst of all is having nobody, except my wretched, decomposing family, who can actually understand what it's like being dead. If I could only send a message, get someone's attention, tell somebody what it's like, then ~~life~~ death would be bearable.

Scarlett lay on her bed, concentrating just hard enough to stop herself sinking through it, and let out a long groan. She was feeling really sorry for herself but wasn't going to allow herself to ghost-cry. Instead, she rolled over and kicked at the wall. Her foot disappeared through the poster for one of her favourite movies, *Sleepy Hollow*. She looked up at the sloping roof above her head, where there were more pictures. Oswald's collection of classic horror-movie posters almost covered the walls of her room. She would have made a really brilliant FX designer if she hadn't died, she thought, and she could have written awesome screenplays and created scary monsters, costumes and make-up that would have won BAFTAs and Golden Globe Awards and Oscar statuettes, for definite. They would have been better than those fake-looking teeth in *Dracula* and with much more realistic blood than *Carrie*. She could have designed scarier bird attacks than Alfred Hitchcock ever did and better werewolf transformations than *American Werewolf in London*. She would have written scripts with more suspense than *Alien*, more jumping-popcorn moments than *Jaws*; scripts that were more creepy than *The Ring* and had more laughs and weird creatures than *Beetlejuice*. I bet I could even invent loads more shocks and cool ways to kill people than *Scream* or *Jeepers Creepers* or *Final Destination*, she decided.

Ghost goss, corpse cringes, death disasters? Swap your sad cemetery stories here

scardeparted:	it's SO unfair! i've got no one to talk to
grimD:	U can talk to me. i don't mind
scarpeparted:	U don't wanna hear my pathetic, girly moaning
grimD:	no probs – really – things'll get better
scardeparted:	yeah, I know. thanks. i kinda miss all the stuff i used to do when i was alive. my friends are gonna do everything without me from now on, aren't they – making videos and everything? i feel SO LONELY!
grimD:	always the hardest thing when you've just kicked the bucket. it'll get easier

scardeparted:	how? are there ghost clubs I can join, y'know, to make friends?
grimD:	U've already got friends
scradeparted:	DUH! i mean ghost-friends, dummy! in case you hadn't noticed, my friends are alive
grimD:	right now they are
scardeparted:	shut up!
grimD:	won't always be ;) and if you miss them THAT much ...
scardeparted:	LOL U R no help at all – what U suggesting? Ha ha! don't even go there! NOT funny – not even slightly funny! signing off now, you lunatic! thanx for making me laugh tho
grimD:	g'night

Scarlett returned to her room, sat on her bed and chuckled. GrimD was such a tease, but at least he'd succeeded in lightening her mood. Yes, having ghost-friends, someone other than just her new chat-room friends, would definitely make death more endurable, but to even consider... What a hilarious suggestion! Not to mention being totally *evil*! He'd said if she missed her friends *that* much, she only had to... But that was the problem. GrimD just didn't understand. She *did* miss them *that* much – so much it hurt like someone had punched her chest and was squeezing her heart. She scrunched up her face and rolled over. The skull on the poster looked down at her again. Scarlett's frown became a smile again, then a grin. She got out a sketch pad and began to jot down some ideas.

Match Day

JP jumped out of bed feeling like an excited kid. So much had happened in the last week. They'd posted their video, he'd been on the telly, Taz had been interviewed and they'd become celebrities. And now he was going to top everything by watching his team play, and beat, Spanswick United. They were going to win. He was certain of it.

It was the first Saturday home match that JP had been able to go to. His mum hadn't let him attend the last two away matches. Both games had been hundreds of miles away across the country and his mum always insisted (unnecessarily, he thought) that the boys, the 'footie crew', should go with an adult, someone else's dad, but nobody had been free. Since JP's own dad had left them when he was a little kid, his mum liked the idea that he would be in the company of a male role model that she approved of. Actually, JP didn't mind so much having to travel to away games with the footie dads, especially if the dad in question had a cool car. And, anyway, the boys had become pretty good at losing their 'dad', often in the car park... after he'd paid for everything, of course.

JP preferred home games. They all did. The matches played at Buttercup Park were a million times better. The Butts' fans loved their home ground. The singing was louder, the chants were funnier and the pies and chips and burgers were tastier. The last home game had been on his gran's sixtieth birthday, so he'd missed that one. But this Saturday afternoon he was going to the Butts versus the Spanners and he couldn't wait.

JP had two groups of friends. There was his best friend Psycho, of course, who he'd known since nursery school, and Rip and Taz (and, until recently, Scar). But Psycho wasn't into football. And the girls, well, they were girls, weren't they? So Jake's other friends were the Butts fans, the footie crew who had always been selected for the school football team without fail every year since

BURGER £2.50
CHEESE BURGER £2.80
DOUBLE BURGER £3.00
BACON BURGER £3.00

BACON ROLL £2.50
BACON + CHEESE £2.80
CHIPS £1
DOUBLE CHIPS £1.60

£2 PIES £2

they were seven or eight, even when he'd started wearing glasses. They were devoted to their local squad, Buttercup Rovers, who practised every week on the field behind Sunshine Street, not far from Jake's house. One day he'd play for them himself, JP decided – if he wasn't in Hollywood making horror movies, of course.

Saturday was perfect, from the moment he got out of bed and saw the cloudless sky, to the free portion of chips he got from the pretty girl in the burger van (because she thought he looked a bit like the Butts' star striker, Lyle Sloggett), to the final score, four–nil (a hat trick from Sloggett and a genius header from Tom Shrubb).

Four–nil!

A perfect day. . . until the crowd began to head home.

JP and his friends weren't sure how it had begun or when things had started to go wrong. One minute they were singing and joking, the next they were jostled in a snarling surge of red faces, confused legs and arms, and yellow football scarves.

It didn't take long for JP to realise that his feet weren't working properly. He took a step with one foot and found the other leg coming with it. His trainer laces were tied together – quite a disadvantage when you were trying not to drown in a stampede of crazed football fans, charging out towards their less-than-happy rivals. Why was the crowd noisier than usual... and much angrier? JP was carried along, powerless, arms pinned to his sides, waiting for the moment when he would stumble and be trampled into the concrete.

It was the pretty girl in the burger van that saved them. They were thrust up against the side of the van and about to go under when she opened the door and dragged the four of them inside. The sound of sirens and police horses could be heard in the distance. The boys peered over the counter at the river of yellow as it reached, and began to mingle with, the ocean of blue.

A blood-chilling sound, the rumble of the feet and fists and angry voices, hit the van and it rocked on its wheels. Buttercup Park had never seen a fight like it. Butts Park was known for its lack of violence, its family atmosphere, its friendly crowd control. They couldn't understand it.

'Look,' said the girl in the van. 'That's why they got angry.' She pointed at the far wall, opposite the home fans' turnstiles. Someone had painted letters, three metres high, in dripping white paint, which read,

SLOGGETT IS A DRUGS CHEAT and a putrid germ!

A strong smell reached their noses. The smell was really odd – out of place; not pies or chips or footie fans' sweat, but the scent of lemons.

'We could have died,' said JP, standing up off the wet bench. He rubbed the back of his damp jeans.

'You're such a drama queen,' said Rip. She pulled the zip on her jacket so that the collar covered her chin. The wind whipped her hair in the air. 'Nobody died. They just got black eyes and split lips.'

'But someone tied my trainers together. I could have been stomped to death.'

'Yeah, right.'

'And did I tell you about the notes?' he continued.

'What notes?' Ripley asked and yawned, clearly bored.

'Someone had stuck notes to people's backs that said stuff like, PUNCH ME, I SUPPORT SPANNERS!'

'On the Butts fans?' said Psycho, coming along the path towards the bench. 'I heard that, too.'

'Yeah,' said JP. 'And notes that said, KICK ME, I'M A SECRET BUTTS FAN! on the Spanswick supporters.'

'I heard they were ruder than that,' said Taz, who was returning from the shop with four bags of crisps and a litre of radioactive-looking bright green fizz.

'Like what?' said Rip.

'Like, kick my butt and spank my spanner,' said Taz, giggling.

'Spank my butt and pinch my bum,' said Rip, shaking with laughter and pulling Taz's sleeve and almost falling over.

'Spin my arse… (*snort*) and poke my dimples… ha ha ha!'

The girls doubled over and cackled uncontrollably, until snot dripped from their noses and their eyes streamed with tears. They'd all caught Rip's cold.

'Dimple my butt hole… (*sniff*) and butter my muffin… ha ha ha!'

'Thanks for the sympathy,' said JP, angrily. He was annoyed, but also confused. It wasn't funny. Something odd had happened at the match. Who had tied his laces together? Who had written that stuff on the wall? He had his suspicions. Something weird was going on, but he didn't know quite what it was. Yet.

The big wooden kitchen table was set for breakfast – a meal none of them would prepare and nobody would eat. The Dedds didn't eat breakfast anymore, but they set the table anyway. Wolfgang pushed his cereal bowl aside and opened a ring-bound lined notebook. He sucked the end of his pen and scratched his head. He scribbled a sentence, froze, scratched his head again, then crossed the sentence out. Amandine sighed and began to hum tunelessly to herself. She stared out of the window. The sound of Milton's skateboard rumbled and clattered along the path at the side of the house, then stopped and rumbled again, far off, in another part of the garden. Scarlett dropped through the ceiling and landed in her chair with a thump.

'Huh,' she grunted.

'What's up?' her dad asked.

'Nothing,' she said. 'Everything. What do you care?'

'Mmm, that's nice.' He wasn't listening. He was writing again.

'What's nice?'

'What you said.'

'I said my life's a disaster and my bedroom's on fire.'

'Are you? That's nice.'

'God, Dad, you're such a loser!'

'Mmm,' Dad agreed.

Scarlett sighed and kicked the table leg. Dad scribbled again. Mum hummed. The skateboard rumble sound changed. There was a muffled growl followed by two seconds of silence, then a crash of splintering wood and glass. Dad crossed out his last scribble.

'Oh, Scarlett,' said Mum, noticing, at last, that her daughter had dropped in. 'Was eet you zat moved zee tin?'

'The tin?' said Scarlett. 'What tin?'

'Zee tin zat was propping up ma chaise. I need eet. I need eet to stop zee silly seeng from falling over. Now eet only 'as sree legs. What use are sree legs?'

'Oh, that tin.'

'*Oui*. Zee tin of paint. White paint.'

'Nah. Wasn't me,' said Scarlett, scratching her nose.

'I will 'ave to steek anuzer book under... aargh!' Mum screamed. 'Meelton! Ma baby! What 'ave you done?'

Milton had pushed open the back door and now stood in the kitchen grinning at them, one half of his broken skateboard in each hand.

'Look,' he exclaimed, nodding at his stomach. 'Cool or what?' A massive splinter of wood, a metre long and as thick as his arm, was protruding from his sweatshirt and shards of glistening glass stuck out of his head like a jagged, diagonal ruffle across his skull. He turned sideways and chortled. 'It goes right through,' he said proudly.

Scarlett was shocked but also fascinated. Her friends in the chat room had been right. Her family all appeared to have quite different ghost-skills and abilities. Milton's were a bit over-theatrical. He was trying out all the dangerous moves he'd been too afraid to attempt when he was alive, and when these extreme activities inevitably ended in a horrible accident, it wouldn't harm him or kill him, just mangle his body in disgusting ways. Well, he was already dead, wasn't he?

Milton's new wooden tail whipped around and clipped the edge of the cooker, making a sickening scrape and squelch sound against his backbone and internal organs. His left kidney fell out and landed with a sticky thump on the kitchen floor.

'I think the greenhouse might be a bit broken,' he added, then walked away.

The faint clickety-click of Wolfgang's keyboard could be heard all through the afternoon and into the night. He'd found inspiration and hadn't typed like this for years. Not since *Pirate in Green Sneakers*. Amandine, too, had discovered her muse. It didn't matter now that her chaise longue had a wobble because she didn't feel the need to lie on it anymore. She hunched instead over her second-hand desk, sketching. The scratchety-scratch of her pencils and drawing nibs joined the clickety keyboard sound as it echoed through the house.

http://scardeparted.blogspot.com

Operation Ghost Friends, Mission #1.
Result: FAILURE.
Glad I didn't try Psycho first, like I wanted, 'cos today was a disaster! Quite humiliating! Total re-think. Rink or school next? Gonna have to research extra-curricular activities.

Ghost goss, corpse cringes, death disasters? Swap your sad cemetery stories here

grimD: don't give up
scardeparted: easy for you to say. U didn't get
                    trampled under a police horse today
                    – was NOT pleasant!

Bunting's Henchmen

In the basement of the Dedds' house, the four friends were making themselves comfortable in their new HQ. It was a lot warmer and drier than the park and relatively comfortable since, so far, their ghost-friend, Scarlett, hadn't tried any more scary stuff.

'You're holding it all wrong,' said JP. 'You gotta rest it on top of your hand, like this.' He grabbed the cue from Ripley and demonstrated the correct snooker grip.

'That's how I was doing it,' she argued.

'No, you weren't. You had it all weird and twisted.'

'You're the one that's weird and twisted.'

'Shut up, you two,' Taz groaned. 'You're givin' me a headache.' She sniffed and poked her new, expensive touch-phone. She was playing a game where you could choose outfits for different characters to wear, then put on a fashion show. She'd told her mum it was a bit childish when Mum had presented it to her the previous evening, but Taz had played it incessantly since she'd loaded it. She sniffed again, then pressed pause and rested the phone on the arm of the sofa while she found a tissue to blow her nose. Taz didn't notice the phone spin around and the screen flick from game mode to calendar.

Psycho was filming the snooker game from different extreme angles: below the table, inside the pockets or with the camera placed directly in the path of the balls. Rip playfully jabbed her cue at his groin and he got the hint. He was getting in her way. He sat down at the other end of the sofa and reviewed the footage. It was quite good. He'd edit it together and add a few transitions and effects. He'd call it *JP playing with Balls* or something. He chuckled, flicked his fringe and stretched his arm across the back of the sofa. None of them saw the tiny puff of dust from the middle cushion – a cloud of dust as if someone had just sat down.

'What was that noise?' said Taz, looking up from the sofa. She'd just blown her nose again on the now-soggy tissue and surreptitiously tucked the pulpy paper wad into a tear on the shabby seat.

'What?' said Psycho.

'I heard something,' said Taz.

'I didn't hear anything,' said Rip. 'You're paranoid.'

'Probably those kids,' said JP.

There had been a group of boys, eight- or nine-year-olds, hanging around at the gate when they'd arrived. The boys had been in the process of rolling two wheelie bins over to the wall so they could climb up and peer over into the Dedds' garden – ghost spotting.

'Izzit the 'ouse what's on YouTube?' one of them had asked.

'Yeah,' JP had replied. 'And the ghosts will rip your horrible throats out if they catch you!'

The boys had run off yelling, 'Hope they get you instead and chop you up in bits!'

'Yeah, and eat your stupid brains!'

Taz looked at the time displayed on her phone. 'Nah. It'll be past their teatime,' she said.

'Past your teatime, you mean,' said Ripley.

'No, s'not,' she protested, touching the screen and scrolling through her calendar. 'But, I have gotta go soon. Flute lesson.'

'Oooooo! A floooot lesson,' said JP. 'How posh.'

'Shut up!'

'Shut up, both of you!' said Psycho. 'I think I heard something that time.'

In the garden, Ivan had just stepped on the remains of the greenhouse. A splinter of glass had pierced the rubber sole of his boot, chopped through his cheesy red acrylic reindeer sock and plunged into the fleshy part of his big toe. Ivan was the size of a large fridge but could be a bit of a baby.

'Aaaaarrrrgghh! Bleedin' gardens. I hate 'em. Should all be concreted over. And the parks.' He hopped on one leg for a bit, carefully tried his weight on the damaged foot, then tried to remember what he'd been saying before their conversation was interrupted. 'Yeah, the best fing abaat knives if they're quiet, right?'

'Yeah, creep up behind 'em, blade between the ribs, give it a twist…' said his smaller but more vicious brother, Vladimir, who was jiggling the handle of the back door. ''Ere, gimme a leg up.'

Ivan limped over and grabbed his brother's raised foot. Vladimir staggered backwards and crashed against the door.

'Oof! I said gimme a leg up, not break my leg!'

'I got a sore foot,' moaned Ivan, pathetically.

'I'll give you a sore face in a minute if you don't stop jigglin' abaat!'

Ivan leaned his massive body forward and rested his shoulder against the wall, while Vladimir stepped into his brother's giant hands and hauled himself on to the sloping roof of the larder. Tiles cracked under Vladimir's knees as he crawled towards the open window of Wolfgang Dedd's study. The sash window was only slightly raised, but it was just enough for him to force his ugly, hairy fingers under and lift it. Below, Ivan grunted as he straightened up to watch his brother flop over the window-sill and disappear inside. Ivan leaned against the wall again and tried to untie his boot. It was quite hard to reach over his enormous gut, so he decided to sit down on the doorstep. He was halfway down when Vladimir opened the kitchen door behind him, from the inside, and Ivan's massive bum shot backwards, propelling both of them across the kitchen floor, where they rolled and landed in a comedy heap under the table.

'There'd better be some serious, quality goods in this Oswald bloke's house,' said Vladimir, rubbing his elbow, 'or I'm gonna be stampin' on that bleedin' sore foot of yours.'

'It IS bleedin', look,' said Ivan, waving a soggy reindeer sock.

The gangsters crept out of the kitchen, across the hallway and up the stairs, leaving a trail of bloody left-foot prints.

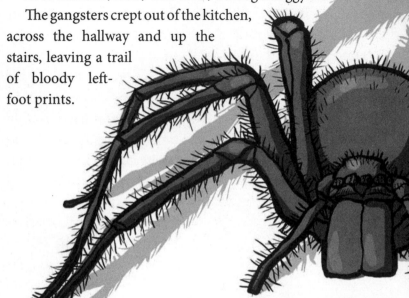

'There,' said Psycho. 'You must have heard that.'

'Scarlett! If that's you,' Ripley shouted. 'That's rubbish haunting. You won't scare anybody with footsteps.'

'Don't wind her up, Rip,' said Taz, looking apprehensive. 'She'll do something freaky-screepy again.'

'You big baby,' said Rip. 'She can't hurt us.'

'How do you know she can't?' said JP.

Another floorboard creaked upstairs, followed by the sound of furniture being moved. Taz cried out in fear, jumped up off the sofa, lost her balance and stumbled forward. She knocked into Rip and sent her staggering into Oswald Dedd's open safe. Glass jars and bottles on the shelves inside rattled and tinkled against each other.

'Hey, watch it, you clumsy plague-wart!' Rip grabbed hold of a shelf and pulled herself up. 'Eeerrr. Have you seen all the weird stuff in here?' She peered at Milton's collection. The safe was crammed with an assortment of glass jam jars, sauce bottles and mustard pots, each with a hand-written label. Milton had thought the safe was a brilliant place to store his samples from the garden. Rip leaned in closer and read,

Alien Bacteeria

on a plastic water bottle containing three dead ants. She picked up a jar beside it and turned it over in her hands.

Mutant Pond Monsta Tenicul

The slimy grey blob resting on the bottom of the jar looked like a slug. It was a slug.

'Eeergh! Repulsive!' Ripley yelled, and dropped the jar back on to the shelf with a clatter. She took hold of the door, which had stood open for years (there being nothing of much value to keep in a safe), and pulled it towards her. The door groaned and coughed out a cloud of rust from the hinges as Rip stepped back, began to push it from the other side, then leaned on it with all her weight and slammed it shut. A note, which had been taped to the front of the door, fluttered to the floor and slipped under the snooker table. It said,

Please DON'T CLOSE THIS
FORGOT THE COMBINATION.

'The safe's not in 'ere either,' said Ivan, coming out of the top-floor bathroom.

'Course it's not, you moron,' said Vladimir. 'What did ya think – he'd hide it under the bath?'

'No. You sure he's got one?' said Ivan, limping after his brother, back down to the first-floor landing.

'Yeah. He told Mr Buntin', didnee: "Please don't hurt me! I'll go home and get your money out of my safe if you promise not to liquidise my fingers."'

'Oh, yeah. I remember. So, d'ya fink he's really got one?'

'Yep, but where is it?'

'What about the whatsit... umm... the thingy, the, y'know, room under the house?'

'The cellar!' yelled Vladimir, grasping his brother around the neck and rubbing the top of his head. 'Clever boy! You're not such a dim-wit after all.'

'Eegh! Vlad! Eegh... I can't... breathe!'

'Come on, then.' Vladimir relaxed his grip and pinched his brother's cheek so hard it left two red blotches.

'What... (*cough*)... What 'bout the ... (*cough*) ... computers and stuff?'

'We'll come back for all that. I want to see some CASH first.'

'Wish 'e 'ad wizzed 'is 'and up in the blender. Wanted to see what it would look like... all crunched up and... blended.' Ivan looked at his own large hand in the gloom and wiggled his fingers, visualising them 'liquidised'.

Vladimir stomped loudly down to the hallway and across the tiled floor to the cellar door. Ivan crept after him on squeaking tip-toes, as quietly as he could in his heavy, rubber-soled boots. He'd put his left one back on but it still pinched a bit and made him wince.

'What you creepin' abaat for?' said Vladimir. 'There's nobody home. It's an empty house.'

'You sure?' Ivan whispered.

'Yeah. The Dedds won't be bothering us,' Vlad chuckled.

'You mean they moved out?'

'You could say they moved out, or you could say they got rubbed out. He he.'

'Oh, right.' Ivan paused, frowned and thought for a moment, then followed his brother down the narrow steps into the basement. 'Wait. What d'you mean?'

'What?'

'Rubbed out?'

'Yeah. Rubbed out.'

'You sayin' they're d-d—'

'You make me laugh, you do,' said Vlad. His brother was hilarious. They'd both spent the afternoon threatening Mr Bunting's 'clients' with extreme acts of violence, but Ivan was getting all wobbly in a house where someone had snuffed it. 'Don't worry. They didn't get gunned down in a hail of bullets or nuffin'. Just ate sumfin' dodgy for their tea.'

They'd reached the den/office/games room. It was very dark and smelled strongly of damp trainers.

'Bingo!' said Vladimir. He'd spotted the safe. 'It's a Pottinger 340. Easy-peasy! We can drill the lock or jelly the 'inges and 'ave it open in no time.'

'Vlad?' whispered Ivan.

'Where's my tool bag?' said Vladimir.

'Vlad, do you hear that noise?' Ivan persisted.

'What noise? Pass the crowbar, will ya?'

'That sorta wheezing noise.'

Vladimir was about to tell his brother to stop being a big, fat, feeble girl but he'd just noticed something, too. He'd spotted an enormous 'thing' lurking in the corner of the room. It was hunched and pulsing in the deep shadows, and made him slightly uneasy. Suddenly, the hideous shape loomed out of the darkness and lurched at them – a monstrous, wheezing, cobweb-covered spectre with bulging, bloodshot eyes, repulsive scaly skin and eight thrashing limbs.

'Rrroooaaahhh!' roared the monster.

The brothers almost wet their pants. They weren't expecting monsters.

'Ahhhhhhh!'

'Get out of my way!'

They ran. Ivan reached the stairs first but Vlad knocked him down and climbed over him, jamming his shoe into his brother's face and gouging a bloody chunk out of his nose, as he frantically clawed himself out of the basement. The monster was gasping and moaning as it dragged its hideous body across the room.

'Don't leave me,' Ivan wailed. He kicked his legs against the steps, but didn't seem to be moving, like a cartoon character running in the air. 'Vlaaaad! M-m-monster's gonna get meeeee!'

At last, his boots made contact with the stairs and he staggered upwards after his brother, who was already halfway down the garden.

JP, Ripley, Taz and Psycho couldn't stop laughing. JP and Ripley dropped the hideous, scaly cushions back on the sofa and Psycho returned the bloodshot eyes to the snooker table, while Taz blew her nose on a new tissue and brushed the cobwebs out of her hair.

'That was brilliant!'

Ghost goss, corpse cringes, death disasters? Swap your sad cemetery stories here

examy:	happy halloween everybody! hey, scardeparted, you feelin' any better?
scardeparted:	yeah, thanx – i sat next to this boy i've always liked today and HE PUT HIS ARM AROUND ME!
examy:	ooo! how lovely! ☺
grimD:	don't encourage her, examy – U know the boy was one of the living and didn't even notice she was there – that's not lovely, it's tragic
scardeparted:	thanx for the support!
examy:	don't listen to him
scardeparted:	i won't

Iced

Taz usually enjoyed her Tuesday afternoon ice-skating lessons, but today, with the flu, she was finding it really hard to skate figures while trying to wipe snot from her sore nose with woollen gloves. The ice rink, on the south side of Buttercup Park, had been quiet when she'd arrived after school, at four, but now it was beginning to fill up with kids: kids who fell down a lot and got in her way.

'Lean forward, over your foot,' said Taz's skating teacher.

'I am,' said Taz, sniffing. Her nose hurt like crazy and she couldn't wait for the lesson to be over.

'No, you're not. Tuck your bottom in.'

'How can I lean forward (*sniff*) *and* tuck my bum in?'

'Now lift your chin up.'

Taz lifted her chin and changed feet, pushing off into the next bend of the figure-of-eight. Out of nowhere, a green padded parka whistled past her.

'Hey!' she yelled and threw her raised leg out to the side, to regain her balance. 'Bottom in!' said her teacher. 'Oh, bottom in in to you, too!' said Taz, rudely. 'Sorry,' she mumbled. 'OK, I think that's enough for today,' said the teacher, looking at her watch. 'Great!' said Taz, as she diverted out of the endless figure-of-eight shape she'd been carving into the ice and dashed off into the crowd. She'd had it with those boring, crappy exercises. She was going to practise her ice dance routine over by the refreshment kiosk, where all the older kids gathered. None of the other teenagers went there to skate. They came to the rink to chat and joke and flirt and snog. The green padded parka whizzed past her again and Taz noticed the girl wearing it. She was pretty and blonde with stick-thin denim legs and chunky white skates that looked brand new. Lucky cow! Taz knew she was just a beginner but could probably fool people into thinking she was a pretty impressive skater because of her dancing skills. She was going to enjoy showing off in front of the growing crowd of popular, cool kids. The green padded parka whizzed past her again, making a big arc. She was at the end of a chain. A chain is when there's a line of people and the one in the middle stands still while the others get swept around the ice. Think of a conker on a string when some hyperactive kid is twirling it around his head, and you'll get the picture. The girl was the conker on the end of the string. The green padded parka swept around the ice. More skaters were joining the chain. There was another. And another. The line was getting longer, until the green parka was somewhere in the middle. The last person to join it, the new conker, was a fat boy wearing a striped jumper. He was now moving at a terrifying speed. Taz was waiting for the rink attendants to step in. Chains on the ice were forbidden. They were fast and dangerous and you could get banned if you started one. Three trips to the sin bin meant a season ban, but if you started a chain, the ban was automatic. She couldn't see any of the rink attendants about. There was no sign of their distinctive red-and-black jackets. It was very strange, Taz thought, because there were always four or five of them on the ice, being total fascists and sending people to the sin bin for eating or sweating or indecent behaviour. Then, as he reached the other end of the circuit and began to head back towards her again, she felt something pushing at her back. Her feet slid forward a few centimetres. 'Don't shove!' she shouted, turning to confront the pusher. There was no one there. The end of the chain swept past her again and she took a step back. It was really zooming now. The boy on the end, Taz noticed, despite his size, looked pale and quite terrified. The nearest person. She tried again to step back, but it was too late. She was several metres away, by the barrier, watching the chain as it continued to rush towards them. There was another heave from the unseen hand and Taz found herself slipping out, right into the path of the oncoming skaters. The boy whooshed at her.

Her sleeve had been grabbed, almost pulling her arm out of its socket, and she was now the last person on the end of the chain.

'Aaahhh!' she yelled. 'Let goooooo!'

The frosty air rushed up her nose and through her hair, making her eyes water and her nose run even more. She was almost blinded and couldn't wipe her face, because one arm was held fast by the fat, striped-jumper boy and the other was thrashing about, keeping her balance. She'd never skated at such a speed before. It was exciting and petrifying at the same time. Should she just hang on and try to enjoy the thrill of whizzing across the ice, she wondered, or should she break herself free and hope to be propelled towards something soft?

She didn't have to make a decision – it was being made for her. All along the line, people began to wobble and trip and tumble into each other. Even the older boy in the middle, the centre of the circle, suddenly sat down heavily on the ice. It was as if someone was running along the chain pushing everyone over. The boy in the striped jumper staggered and released Taz's arm. She was free at last, able to put her hand up to wipe her eyes.

When she peeked through her woollen fingers, she shrieked. She was still travelling at a terrific speed, straight for the barrier and the group of teenagers by the kiosk. She had to stop somehow or she'd smash into the wooden wall and end up a bloody pile of broken bones and mush. What was the best way to stop?

Could she try the jump she'd been working on, a toe loop? She had no time to think about how dangerous it might be at this speed. She'd try it. She shifted her weight, turned, reached back with a straight left leg, picked the ice with her left toe, bent her knees and swung around, her arms tucked in, to land on the right, back, outside edge, arms out for balance and a final flourish.

Leap... thump... shhhhhh!

She landed awkwardly and stopped, sending a spray of ice and water over the barrier and all over her stunned audience. It was probably the scariest thing she'd ever tried but she'd done it! A slightly less than perfect landing, but at least she'd stopped. She grinned, then lost her balance, wobbled and fell backwards on to her bum. 'Oof!'

If you've relaxed, thinking that she was now safe, if a little bruised and embarrassed, then you'd better think again.

'Look out!' someone shouted from over by the kiosk.

Taz looked up from behind her scarf, where she had been trying to hide her red face. A chaotic wall of skaters seemed to be rushing straight towards her. The chain had broken apart, but there was enough velocity in those still upright to propel them out in all directions in a dangerous explosion of legs and arms, padded coats and lace-up boots – boots with blades attached!

Taz closed her eyes, held her breath and waited for the thump of impact and the slice of metal through her body. She felt a whoomp of air rushing past and heard the clatter of boots and blades and limbs as the skaters smashed into each other and the barrier.

Then silence.

She opened her eyes.

She was alive.

'Get up!' a voice yelled from the crowd.

Taz breathed again then began to rummage in her pocket for a tissue.

'Move, you moron!' shouted another voice.

Taz couldn't find the tissue. It must have fallen out during her lesson or her spectacular leap. She smiled to herself. It was probably the best jump she'd ever done. Her teacher had been right about keeping her weight over her foot and bending her knees. If she wasn't too bruised, she was going to have another go at it. She'd just get her composure back and wait for her pulse rate to drop a bit, then she'd really impress everyone by doing it again. Without falling over.

The other bruised and battered skaters from the chain were getting to their feet and stumbling towards the exits, some cradling damaged limbs or dabbing at bloody grazes.

'Get out of the way!' Someone was still yelling. Who were they shouting at, Taz wondered?

'Taz, get off the ice!' screamed Ripley. Taz recognised the voice this time. She looked over to the barrier and saw her friends, Ripley, JP and Psycho. Psycho was pointing his video camera at her while the other two were frantically waving their hands.

'Hiya,' she called and waved back. She could hear a strange rumble and the ice beneath her seemed to be vibrating, but her bum wasn't too numb with cold yet so she was going to take her time getting up.

'Move, you idiot!' JP shouted.

'What?' Taz was confused. 'What for?'

'That!' the trio screamed, pointing across the rink.

She looked over her shoulder and the fleeing skaters parted to reveal the cause of the panic. It was the giant ice-resurfacing machine and it was about to spread frozen Taz across the ice.

'That was close,' said Ripley, rewinding the footage on Psycho's camera once again. The ice-resurfacing machine travelled rapidly backwards, away from Taz, then she pressed a button and it went forwards again. She had only just got out of the way in time.

'D'you think it was an accident?' said JP.

'What do you mean?' said Taz. 'Duh! Course it was an accident.'

'So, who called all the rink attendants to a fake staff meeting and then locked them in the office?'

'I dunno.'

'Who started the chain?'

'Some older boy, probably. Him and his friends,' said Taz. What JP had said was starting to worry her. She wanted to ask who *he* thought had pushed her into the path of the chain, but didn't dare.

'Who started up the ice-resurfacing machine and let off the hand-brake?'

'Who would do something THAT stupid?' said Ripley.

'I'm not sure, but I have an idea,' said JP. 'Do you smell lemons?'

'Hot dog?' Psycho asked, returning from the kiosk with their food orders.

'Yeah. Thanks,' said JP, quietly, deep in thought. He'd smelled lemons before, at the match.

'Chips with ketchup for you, Rip.'

'Thanks.'

'Pizza slice for me and here's your ice-cream, Taz.'

'Did you remember the chocolate sprinkles and *no nuts*?'

'Yeah. I get it. You don't like nuts,' said Psycho.

'If I eat nuts, I'll swell up and stop breathing and drop down dead!'

'Really?' said Ripley. 'I'd like to see that. It would be kinda entertaining.'

'Shut your face!' Taz grabbed the cone of chocolate ice-cream and was about to take a lick. 'Is this a joke?' she asked, staring at it.

'What?' Psycho asked, his mouth full of pepperoni.

'It's not funny!' she shouted and rammed the ice-cream into Psycho's chest.

'Hey!'

'Nuts!' said Taz and stamped off on her skates, disappearing into the crowd.

'What's she on about? She's gone mental,' said Psycho, prising the ice-cream off his jacket. He glanced down and froze. 'Oh, no! There *are* nuts on it.' He looked at the others. 'But I put sprinkles on, not nuts. I didn't touch the nuts, honest.'

16

The Twins

Scarlett was furious. Furious and exhausted. That was the second occasion one of her friends was on their own in a location with accident potential, and she'd failed again. She'd worked so hard on Mission #2: Ice Taz. The research. The timings. But everything had gone wrong, even Plan B and Plan C. She couldn't believe it. She pushed angrily through a group of startled children, who were playing at being zombies emerging out of piles of leaves, then felt another putrid vomit-belch rumble up from her stomach.

'Oooo,' she moaned. 'No more.'

'Watcha, poo-stripe!' yelled a voice behind her. She turned to find her brother Milton dangling from a tyre swing in the play area with a giant, mischievous grin on his face.

'Get lost, maggot-boy!' said Scarlett.

'You stink of puke,' said Milton.

'Well you are puke! Puke and maggots!'

'I know you are, so what am I?'

'Shut up!'

'Shaaat aaap!' Milton sang.

'Milt?' Scarlett asked. She'd just noticed that something wasn't quite right with Milton's midsection. 'What have you done?'

'What d'ya mean?'

'Your middle. What is that?'

Milton wriggled free of the tyre and floated to the ground. The jagged remains of the broken greenhouse had now gone, but something equally horrific seemed to have happened to his ten-year-old body.

'Oh, you mean this? Playing chicken.'

'What?'

'Are you deaf as well as dumb and pukey? Play-ing chick-en. In the High Street. Wasn't fast enough getting out the way of a bus.'

Scarlett gasped as her brother turned sideways and showed her what the bus had done. Milton's body was squashed flat across the middle and he had deep bus tyre-tracks embossed on his stomach. 'Eerrgh! That's disgusting!'

'It'll pop back, 'cos I done it before, but I like it. Look.' He flapped his arms at her. They were squashed flat, too. 'Yesterday, I train-surfed on the Tube and got splatted into jam on a bridge. I stayed jam all day. Walked about like a big, wobbly gore-jelly. It was so cool!'

'It's not cool; it's repulsive, you freak.'

'Who you calling a freak? Anyway, it was sweet. My brain popped out and everything.'

'Urgh!' said Scarlett. 'You need to see a doctor, pronto.'

'Too late for that.'

Scarlett sniggered. Milton could actually be quite funny for a maggot-boy, she thought. Milton climbed back into the tyre and Scar sat on the roundabout. It was starting to get dark and people were going home. Mums with buggies were grabbing their toddlers and dog-walkers were doing a final trudge around the park and scooping up squishy piles of their dogs' poo in little plastic bags. Yuck! Across the play area, Scarlett could see two pairs of legs, dangling from the climbing tree. The tree was old and sagging and perfect for climbing, but it was also surrounded by a rusty metal railing and decorated with a load of signs that said,

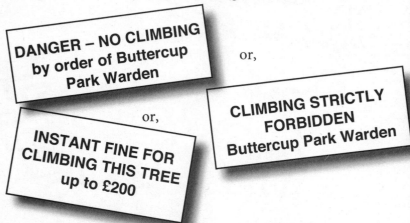

DANGER – NO CLIMBING
by order of Buttercup
Park Warden

or,

or,

INSTANT FINE FOR
CLIMBING THIS TREE
up to £200

CLIMBING STRICTLY
FORBIDDEN
Buttercup Park Warden

It was sign overkill, Scarlett thought. She couldn't quite see who had ignored the signs and climbed the tree, because they were hidden in the branches and the tree was desperately hanging on to the last of its dry, brown leaves. All she knew was that they were rule-breakers and wore colourful striped socks, and for those reasons she definitely liked them.

'That's Brian and Barbara,' said Milton, jumping on to the roundabout and making it spin and tilt and scrape the ground.

'In the tree?' Scarlett asked. 'How do you know?'

'I know everyfink 'bout the park. They're twins. They're our neighbours. They live in that black and white house, over there.' He pointed at a large, detached house at the end of Moonlight Street, the road that ran back-to-back with Sunshine Street.

'I've never seen them before,' said Scar.

'They're here every day,' said Milton, hanging off the now rapidly-spinning roundabout with one hand.

'Must go to the other school,' Scarlett mumbled, thoughtfully.

'Don't think they go to school.' Milton let go of the handrail and flew head first into the concrete with a crunch. Scarlett lost sight of him as the roundabout turned. When she had done the full circuit, Milton was back on his feet scrutinising his latest injury. He had a long, bloody gash down his face and neck where the skin had peeled off like an orange. Further down, a grizzly, jagged, broken thigh bone was protruding from his leg.

'Brilliant! Look at that!' he cried. 'I'm gonna go and scare Mum with it.' He floated away, across the playing field.

'Maggoty mush-brain!' Scarlett called after him.

'Stinky toilet-breath!' he replied.

Scarlett detached herself from the roundabout and floated above it, feeling dizzy. She glanced over at the climbing tree again. Now that she'd changed position, she could just make out the shapes of Brian and Barbara in the gloom. She soared upwards. The twins looked exactly alike and about the same age as her. The rest of their clothes, like their socks, were amazing. Really different. In fact, Scarlett thought she might have seen a jumper like the girl was wearing in a charity shop. She was delighted. Brian and Barbara wore second hand! The girl was frowning while reading a book and the boy was flicking an orange yo-yo up and down. Scarlett smiled to herself. So what if her latest plan at the ice rink hadn't worked? She'd try again and think of something more ingenious next time. And now she had two more names for her hit list – Brian and Barbara.

Scarlett floated through the back door and across the kitchen. She could hear voices in the conservatory.

Milton was probably giving Mum a fright with his grizzly injuries, she thought. Then she heard Dad's voice, too. She crossed the hall and eased her head through the conservatory door. What she saw inside was both surprising and confusing. Milton was standing on the wobbly chaise longue, riding it like a surfboard, with his arms outstretched, while Mum sat at her desk doing a sketch of him, not freaked out at all by his protruding leg bone. Dad had apparently abandoned his office and had brought his chair and laptop downstairs to set himself up opposite Mum at her desk. They seemed to be having a terrific time. Scarlett was astonished.

'What are you doing?' she asked.

'Hi, Scarlett!' said Dad. 'Have you seen Milt's leg? Great, isn't it?'

'You've all gone mental,' said Scarlett, pushing the rest of her body through the door. 'It's the strain of being corpses, isn't it?'

'He cut zee top of ees head off yesterday,' said Mum, pointing to the gruesome sketch evidence, taped to the wall.

'You're all bonkers!' Scarlett backed out into the hall again. She started to drift up the stairs. She couldn't believe how pathetic her family was. They were sick freaks and she needed to get as far away from their lunacy as possible. She would lock herself in her room and listen to Si Storm at full volume.

Ghost goss, corpse cringes, death disasters? Swap your sad cemetery stories here

scardeparted:	is there a way to get my family committed to a ghost mental asylum? i think the pathologist forgot to put their brains back after the autopsies
toxicboy:	U'R lucky to have a dead family – mine are still alive
grimD:	as, it appears, are all scardeparted's friends
toxicboy:	so the peanut allergy thing didn't work, then?
scardeparted:	no
grimD:	actual poison is more effective – less chance they'll pull through
scardeparted:	i'm not g

She stopped typing.

What was that?

There were voices in the house. She listened. They were coming from the cellar. Her annoyingly-still-alive friends were down there again.

She sank through the floor.

'Do you think those boys will come back?' asked Taz.

'Nah, we gave them a brown-trousers fright,' said Ripley, giggling.

'I don't think they were boys, though,' said JP. 'Looked like blokes to me.'

Psycho put down his video camera. 'Blokes?'

Scarlett knew exactly who they'd been. Of course it hadn't been boys. She'd heard Vladimir and Ivan breaking in and had followed them around the house, from room to room, all the while trying to come up with a really clever way to get them out. She'd heard them talking about her uncle, what they thought he might have hidden in his safe and what gruesome things they'd been planning to do to him. They'd not seen her, of course. Nor had they spotted Dad dozing in an armchair in his office, nor Mum arranging her drawing inks, in colour order, in the conservatory. Then, before Scarlett could put her plan into action – to slam some doors and frost the windows a bit (give her a break, it *was* short notice) – they had gone into the basement. Scarlett felt totally disgraced. Her friends had done a brilliant scare-job, much more effective than her idea, and they weren't even dead!

'You didn't scare some little kids, you stupid morons!' Scarlett yelled at them. 'They're psychopathic thugs!'

It was pointless. They couldn't hear her. She looked down at Taz's mobile, resting again on the arm of the sofa, and considered texting her. She reached out her hand. Urgh, no! She'd probably throw up again and she'd only just recovered from being a giant puke fountain after the ice rink. It wasn't worth the mess or the discomfort. She slumped down on the sofa.

'Forget the blokes. We need to talk about something,' said JP.

'What?' said Ripley. 'You mean your dumb Scarlett theory?'

'It's not dumb.' Psycho sat down right on top of Scarlett, giving her a shock and a strange, squishy sensation that was actually quite nice.

'You think *Scarlett* put the nuts on my ice-cream,' said Taz.

Scarlett had had enough. They were going to guess what was going on at any moment and she had to distract them. Perhaps she could get them to think about the gangsters again. She disengaged herself from Psycho, wondering if passing through his body was actually the most intimate and sexy thing she'd ever experienced. She shivered, then whooshed upstairs and opened the front door.

SLAM!

'What was that?' said Taz.

'They're back,' said JP. 'Looking for stuff to steal.'

Result, thought Scarlett, and punched the air with her fist. Now she just had to give them another hint. How could she warn her friends that these men were dangerous? They'd be back with guns and knives and power tools sharpened to points that would cause maximum damage and pain to their victims. They were violent torturers and *killers*.

Wait! Killers? Scarlett scratched her ghost-head. What was she worried about? If Vladimir and Ivan came back and caught her friends in the house they might... no, she couldn't possibly want *that*... could she?

'Well, next time we'll be ready for them,' said Ripley.

'Yeah, you're right. We've got all the equipment. Let's make it our most impressive horror project yet,' said Psycho.

'A proper monster or a ghost to frighten them away forever.'

17

The Deep End

Psycho looked at the screen of his phone.

scars @ 8 brng
FX stff
ip

He snapped it shut and tucked it inside his rolled-up clothes, then stuffed them all into his locker. He was late for the last Wednesday swim club meeting at Buttercup Park pool, housed in an old and run-down building, built in the fifties, with peeling paint, drafty changing rooms and a boiler that kept breaking down. Buttercup Park pool was shunned by more discerning local residents who preferred to make the twenty-minute trip to a shiny new leisure complex over in the next district. The swim club met there because it was cheap and they could have the place virtually to themselves.

'Chop, chop, Mr Flint,' called the swimming coach.

Psycho jogged to join the other boys shivering beside the starting blocks at the deep end.

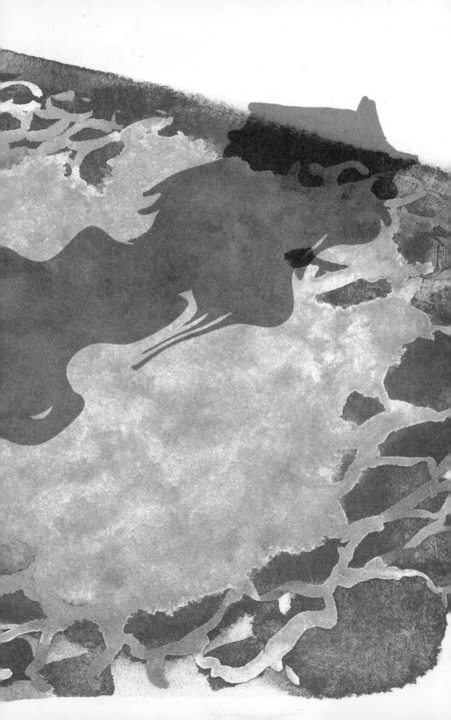

'Your dead girlfriend make you forget what time it was, Psych?' whispered Matt Pickle, the club's star freestyle swimmer. 'She just lie there, all stiff and lifeless? Ha, ha! Does she let you do things to her? Get a good feel of her dead body, did ya?'

'You're sick,' said Psycho.

'Finish warm-up stretches, please, then I want two hundred metres, against the clock,' said the coach and he blew his whistle.

Psycho jumped. There was no reason to blow his whistle, he thought. The coach just did it for emphasis, like punctuation. Or just to annoy them. Psycho stretched down and tried to touch his toes, then stood up and flopped his arms over his head. He groaned. That was enough stretching.

'On your marks,' said the coach. 'Set...' He whistled again.

The water was like ice, but after pounding up and down the pool eight times, it didn't feel so bad. For the rest of the hour, they practised starts and relay change-overs. Psycho was the last to get out of the water. He put his hands on the side and pulled himself up, then picked up his towel and followed the others into the changing room. The boiler had broken down again and the boys were huddled around a large fan-heater in the corner. The machine wasn't making much difference to the arctic temperature in the cubicles, but it was better than nothing.

'Coach?' asked Psycho. 'Can I stay a bit longer?'

'Sure,' said the coach. 'You wanna practise that backstroke turn?'

'Yeah. Regatta's only three months away and I think I could win it this year.'

'Yrrrrr,' chorused the rest of the team. It sounded like a jeer but the boys were actually agreeing with him. He could win the two-hundred-metre backstroke, if he could judge the turn better.

'I've left my thermos in my car,' the coach explained to Psycho, rubbing his hands together as another draft whistled through the changing room. The boys had thrown on their clothes and were now trooping out the door. 'Got some hot soup, so I'll just pop out. Don't get in the pool 'til I get back. OK?'

'OK.'

Psycho trudged back out to the pool. He was the best backstroke swimmer in the club, but had come second in the two-hundred-metres at the Sports Centre Regatta three years running. It was frustrating and he didn't think he could bear to fail again. He knew he could do better and he could show that worm Pickle that he wasn't a loser. He stood on the edge of the pool.

'Hey, Psych!' yelled Matt Pickle from the changing room. 'See ya next week – if you don't go and drown yourself to be wiv your girlfriend.'

Psycho walked along the edge, backwards, circling his arms and counting. At the end he reached out, touched an imaginary wall and turned to face the other way. The coach wasn't back yet. How long did it take to get to the car park and back? Perhaps he'd popped in to see the pool manager. Psycho had noticed him earlier, when he'd arrived, hunched in his office beside the front entrance. The office looked quite cosy, so the coach was probably taking his time, having a cup of tea. He couldn't wait for him all night. The water might be warmer than the air. He jumped in, swam to the middle lane, kicked out to the centre of the pool and waited.

Then something moved at the deep end. Psycho ran his hand over his eyes and looked again. There was something on the edge of the pool. Something that hadn't been there earlier. It looked a bit like a pile of white towels. Perhaps the coach was back and he'd brought them. But it wasn't towels, it was a box or... Psycho swam nearer, then stopped.

A fan heater!

It was the fan heater from the changing room! The fan heater had a tail. There was a white cable hanging from the back, which curled down on to the tiles and trailed along the side of the pool where it plugged into an extension box and became an orange cable that ran all the way into the changing rooms. Psycho changed direction.

Swim away!

No, not just swim away, he had to get out of the pool, FAST!

He plunged his hands into the water and kicked his legs frantically. He looked back. The heater was edging forward. He was on his front but knew he could be faster on his back. Should he roll over and change strokes, he wondered. No, just get out, you bloody idiot!

GET OUT NOW!

He was an arm's length from the side. He stretched and reached, but felt nothing, only water. Not an arm's length. He'd misjudged the distance. Perhaps that was why he couldn't get his turns right. One more stroke. He touched the side at last, grabbed and hauled himself up. His arms ached from the exertion but he found the strength from somewhere and crawled on to the tiles as, over his shoulder, he saw the heavy fan-heater topple into the water.

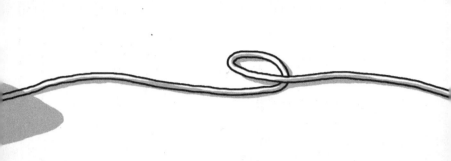

He'd made it just in time! He blew out his cheeks with relief and looked down at the water.

Wait! The water wasn't fizzing or crackling or lit up, like in a movie. Nothing had happened. The air should have been filled with the tangy scent of pool-sized electrolysis – like the experiment they'd done in chemistry, running a current through water. Or perhaps the pungent aroma of boiled Goth! He was standing in a puddle at the pool's edge, still linked to the water. So he should have been flapping about like a gasping fish, with hundreds of volts buzzing through his body. Shouldn't he?

Then a thought popped into his head, like a light bulb switching on. Circuit-breakers. His dad was always moaning on about using circuit-breakers with drills and hedge-trimmers and the lawnmower. Dad was a lawyer, not an electrician (or a gardener), but a lawyer who was a bit of a drippy safety nerd. His dad had said a circuit-breaker could save one of their lives one day and he had been right.

'Stinking, flesh-eating plague-virus!' That had given him a fright. He shivered like someone had walked over his grave and then went into the changing room. Perhaps JP was right. Could they all be targets? He had to warn the others – text them. He took a step towards his locker and lost contact with the floor.

'Woah!' he yelled, as his feet slipped and slithered in different directions. He danced and slid across the changing room, surfing the tiles, then rammed his shoulder into the hard edge of a metal locker and landed in a heap. The locker door popped open above him and a pair of blue flippers landed on his head. 'Ouch!' A little stunned, he rubbed his head and sat up. His hand left a slick of something sticky in his hair. It smelled like... It smelled like his shampoo. He was covered in it. Someone had emptied his bottle of shampoo all over the floor. There was another smell, too. It was really strong. The smell of lemon and bleach.

He jumped at the car-crash sound of metal against metal. The locker by the door had toppled and rammed into the one next to it and, one after another, the heavy steel, coffin-shaped boxes fell, like dominoes, heading inexorably towards him. His feet skittered and slithered again as he grappled with the long, wooden bench and leaped out of the way as the final locker slammed on to the tiles behind him.

'Hey, Scarlett!' he shouted, angrily. He didn't think he liked her anymore, now that she'd tried to kill him. 'What did you do that for? Think you could break my skull, did you? I've got a hard head. Bet you forgot about circuit-breakers, too. You can't get me that easily, you know. You'd better watch out, 'cos we're on to you now and we're REALLY PISSED OFF!'

'Very amusing,' said the coach, who was standing in the doorway frowning at him.

'Amusing?' said Psycho. 'What's amusing about getting murdered?'

'Murdered? Ha! Tell ya mates I'll murder them if they try a prank like that on me again. Locking me out? Very funny. Locking those doors is a fire hazard, you know. I had to break a window, which you lads are gonna pay for, I might add. And clear up this mess before you go.'

Operation Ghost Friends, Mission #3.
Result: COMPLETE FAILURE.

Ghost goss, corpse cringes, death disasters? Swap your sad cemetery stories here

scardeparted:	i think i've made a huge mistake
examy:	still puking?
scardeparted:	not so much but it's not that – i made him h8 me!
examy:	what happened? last time we chatted, you'd just had a sexy thru-bod experience with him, right?
scardeparted:	but I've ruined it all now – i'm a terrible person – what was i thinking?
examy:	i'm sure he doesn't h8 U
grimD:	he won't h8 you when U'R all together again, making awesome horror movies… and having real ghost-bod experiences!!
scardeparted:	U R disgusting!

JP's phone beeped and vibrated in his pocket. He got down from the chair he'd been standing on in the Dedds' hallway, dropped the coil of nylon rope on the floor and plunged his hand into the back of his jeans. It was a text from Psycho.

'Boil-pus! She got Psycho at the pool,' he said.

'He's not dead, is he?' Ripley crawled out from under a table.

'Yeah, right. He's dead and he just texted me. Duh! Course he's not dead.'

'Who's dead?' asked Taz, wandering into the hallway.

'Psycho. But he's not dead. Scar tried to kill him, that's all,' said JP.

They'd been at the Dedds' house for almost an hour but none of their effects were completely set up yet. Psycho was bringing some equipment, so they'd done as much as they could for now. Ripley and JP decided to play a game of snooker while they waited. They trudged downstairs to the basement.

They agreed to the best of three, but started an argument by the end of the first game.

'You're such a cheat,' said JP.

'I did not cheat. I just moved the ball back. You're allowed to do that, aren't you, Taz?'

Taz was slumping on the sofa, playing with her hair. She shrugged.

'Those might be the rules on your planet, but…' JP began.

'I'm not playing anymore. I'm going to explore.' Ripley stamped up the stairs.

JP looked at Taz. He was confused. 'What was that all about?'

'Nervous about her speech tomorrow?' Taz shrugged again then got up and went to look for her friend. She found her poking around in the conservatory.

'You know when we came last time?' Ripley asked. 'Did you see all *these* in this glass room thingy?' She was waving some of Amandine Dedd's sketches.

'It's a conservatory, brain-damage,' said Taz.

'Whateva.'

'It's really old and not a proper conservatory, like at our house, but that is what it's called,' said Taz.

'Yeah, OK, not interested. Look,' said Rip. 'I'm sure these weren't here before.' She held up the sketch of Milton 'surfing' on the chaise longue so that Taz could see it.

'They must have been here last time,' said Taz. 'You just didn't notice.'

'I would have noticed this.' Ripley pulled out another drawing. It was an ink sketch of Milton impaled on iron railings, the spikes piercing his body like a comb through hair.

'Hey!' said Taz, laughing. 'That's really cool!'

'But I think it's a picture of Scarlett's little brother,' said Rip.

'Yeah, you're right,' said Taz. 'Scar's mum was a bit of a sicko!'

'Super-size sicko! If they weren't dead, we'd have to call Social Services, right? This

one is even sicker.' She showed Taz another sketch.

Eventually, JP tired of playing snooker on his own and joined the girls upstairs. They were still flicking through Amandine's scary sketchbooks and Wolfgang's notes when Psycho arrived.

'Psych, mate,' said JP as Psycho walked into the conservatory. 'Come and look at this.'

'Don't you wanna know how close I came to dying?' Psycho asked.

'Yeah, later,' said Ripley, not even raising her head.

'Cheers,' said Psycho with a sigh. 'I survived attempted murder and you're not interested.'

'We're bored with all that,' said Taz. 'Being murdered is SO last week.'

'But she electrocuted me!' yelled Psycho.

'That explains your twisted, ugly face then,' said JP.

'And that smell,' said Ripley with a snigger, though she didn't feel like laughing. She'd just realised she was the only one left.

Was she next on the list for a strange accident? Would Scarlett try to kill her, too?

Psycho was also thinking about Scarlett. He'd been reliving his terrifying, death-cheating ordeal in his head, over and over again, all the way back from the pool. But his friends didn't seem to care or hear what had happened. He sighed and rummaged in his school bag. 'So, where d'you want the webcam?' he asked.

Psycho had brought all his electronic gadgets, so they were now able to get on with setting up the FX. It took much longer than they'd hoped. Probably because Rip's bad mood got worse and she and JP argued again. They got back to their homes really late, way past the usual school-night curfew.

None of them slept well. Unsettling nightmares of bodies impaled on railings, rabid football crowds, bone-crushing ice-resurfacing machines and killer fan-heaters churned through their dreams all night, causing them to wake stressed and tired.

Rip 4 Prez

Ripley was especially annoyed at her lack of sleep and the dark circles under her eyes. She illegally texted Taz during the first lesson of the morning. Taz met her in the girls' loos at break with her make-up bag, as requested.

'Awww,' Ripley moaned, staring at herself in the mirror. 'I look like Scarlett. How can I make a speech to the whole canteen at lunch, looking like a decomposing corpse?'

'Here,' said Taz, handing her a tube of concealer.

At twelve thirty, Ripley dashed out of Mr Carver's history classroom before the bell stopped ringing and within seconds was handing out leaflets at the door to the canteen.

This is what they looked like:

RIPLEY MUCHMORE
4 SCHOOL PREZ
My Pledge
Vote for me and I promise to:

* negotiate a 'Fashionable Uniform Agreement'
(no more short-skirt Gestapo!)
* lobby for more choice in the canteen
(no more vats of pea and pig soup!)
* insist on the return of all confiscated items
(give us back our skull rings!)
* be a sympathetic listener, a passionate advocate and a benevolent President
VOTE 4 RIP next week
because I really care :-)

'What took you so long? I've been here for hours,' Rip whined, as Taz trotted towards her down the corridor, carrying a heavy cardboard box. She was out of breath.

'Didn't you hear? (*puff*) Something happened in the teacher's car park and the Headmaster called the fuzz.'

'Fan-tastic!' said Rip, sarcastically. 'The whole stupid school will be rubber-necking out there instead of listening to my speech.' She looked over at the temporary stage and lectern that had been constructed on the other side of the canteen. Both of the candidates were to address the school at one o'clock, but the room was almost empty and it was twenty to one.

'Don't freak out,' Taz reassured her. 'They won't miss their nosh just 'cos the plods are nicking somebody.' As if to prove her point, a group of hungry-looking younger kids jostled through the double doors and Ripley thrust her leaflets into their hands.

'Badges, badges!' she hissed at Taz.

'Oh, yeah.' Taz remembered the cardboard box in her arms and dropped it on a nearby table. She ripped it open to reveal hundreds of tiny badges that looked like this:

Taz ran after the kids and gave each of them a badge while Ripley fixed her face into a perfect, politician-style smile which she beamed at a group of approaching older girls.

'We're voting for Max,' said one of the girls.

'Yeah, Max Rocket is a hottie,' said the girl next to her.

'We lurve him,' said the first.

Refusing to be discouraged, Ripley grabbed a handful of badges, distributed them and smiled again.

'You got any with some other design?' asked the third girl.

'Yeah, got any with hearts or swear words on?' asked the fourth.

'No. Duh! They're my badges,' said Rip, losing her patience at last. 'Why would I have swear words on my School President campaign badges?'

'OK. We were only asking,' said the first girl. 'You hormonal, or what?'

'You must be total thickies to be voting for Max Rocket,' Rip mumbled. She was trying to regain control and stay calm. The girls flicked their long hair at her and walked away. 'He's the stupidest person on the planet,' she called after them. 'And, anyway, who'd vote for someone with a name that sounds like a porn star?'

The girls strutted over to the salad counter.

'Thought you didn't approve of negative campaigning,' said a voice behind her. 'You're not s'posed to just slam your opponent, you know,' said JP. He grinned at her.

'Jake, it's all a big, fat, oozing disaster,' Ripley moaned. 'Complete bio-hazard! Look at my audience.'

'A couple of junior germs and a few A-star sluts.' JP scanned the canteen. 'I see what you mean.'

'Go to the teachers' car park and round them up,' Rip begged him. 'Pleeeaase!'

'Why the teachers' car park?' said JP frowning. 'They're behind the gym.'

'But I thought the pigs were here because some yob scratched a teacher's car, or something?'

'Nah, I heard a van-load of sports equipment's gone missing.'

'You're both wrong,' said Psycho

walking towards them with his video camera. 'Fuzz are investigating a kitchen break-in.'

'I don't care!' Ripley yelled. 'Please just go and drag them in here! Give them food, money, your body, whatever! Just GET ME SOME VOTERS!'

Ripley's last four words echoed around a silent room. Everyone had suddenly stopped talking. The junior germs, the sluts and the canteen staff had all turned to face the doors where two uniformed police officers now stood. Rip blushed bright red and stepped back to allow them access. The whole school seemed to be shuffling in behind them, murmuring. Then there was a commotion in the kitchen: the sound of a muffled argument followed by the clang of a large pan hitting the floor.

'I hope that was the pea and pig soup,' hissed Taz.

The Headmaster emerged from the kitchen, a concerned look on his face, and joined his Deputy and the police officers for a whispered discussion. Then they all disappeared back into the kitchen.

'Nothing to worry about,' called the Deputy Head, nervously, as she went through the door. 'Candidate speeches will take place as planned, so carry on.'

The canteen erupted into an excited buzz of chatter and Ripley was relieved to see that all the pupils were now joining the lunch queue and settling down at the tables to eat. She had her voters. Taz and JP helped her to hand out more badges and leaflets, then Rip fixed her smile again and set off around the room to speak to every student, followed by Psycho and his camera. Eventually, she strode back towards her pals, who were now waiting for her by the stage. Her face was creased into an angry frown.

'God, this school is full of putrid, imbecile knuckle-draggers,' she growled. 'Half-wit scumbags who only care about one thing.

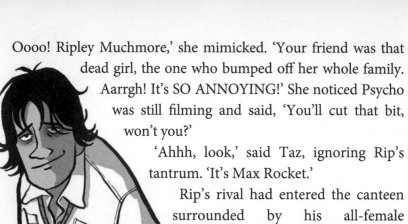

Oooo! Ripley Muchmore,' she mimicked. 'Your friend was that dead girl, the one who bumped off her whole family. Aarrgh! It's SO ANNOYING!' She noticed Psycho was still filming and said, 'You'll cut that bit, won't you?'

'Ahhh, look,' said Taz, ignoring Rip's tantrum. 'It's Max Rocket.'

Rip's rival had entered the canteen surrounded by his all-female entourage. He was going to be a hard person to beat, but Ripley was satisfied that she'd researched exactly what the pupils really wanted and had done heaps more campaigning than Max. In fact, Max hadn't done any at all. He thought securing votes was like adding friends to his social-networking account, and everyone wanted to be Max Rocket's friend, didn't they?

Following behind Max was Destiny Proudfoot, the current School President and Ripley's idol.

'I was just telling Max,' said Destiny. 'I'll introduce you, then you each get ten minutes and I'll chair a Q&A at the end. OK?'

Ripley gulped. She thought Destiny was awesome but had no idea what she'd just said. What on earth was 'akewanay'? Something they would do after their speeches. What could it be? Then she suddenly worked it out and flushed red again. Destiny meant that there would be *questions and answers* at the end. Rip was such a bug-brain! She blew out her cheeks and tried to gather her thoughts. Keep it together, she told herself. Destiny was on the stage and testing the microphone.

'Hello, hello. Ladies, gentlemen, fellow students and teachers,' she began. 'As your School President…' A few half-hearted cheers bubbled up from the diners, together with a couple of obscene hand-gestures. '…it is my great honour to introduce the two presidential candidates, one of whom shall take my place. Today they will each be telling you why you should vote for them next week.' At this point, Destiny put her hand over the microphone (which made the speakers emit a horrible screeching noise) and turned to Ripley. 'You going first?' she asked.

'Y-y-yeah,' said Rip, her stomach dropping down into her shoes.

'Will you give a round of applause for the first candidate, Millie Lotsmore,' announced Destiny.

Rip climbed the three steps on to the stage with legs that felt like cooked spaghetti. She was trembling. Even acting in the school play hadn't been as terrifying as this. She moved towards the lectern and unfolded the two sheets of paper on which she'd printed her speech. The paper crackled in her shaking hands and the microphone amplified the sound around the room. Oh, help, she thought. This is a truck-load of super-scary! And what is that disgusting, lemony-bleach smell? She cleared her throat and began, 'Actually, it's Muchmore, Rip—'

Weeeeeeeooooooooweeee

The fire alarm siren wailed through the building. The Deputy Head walked briskly into the canteen again, this time with three other teachers at her heels. Her voice was barely audible over the siren.

'Stop eating! Everyone move quickly and quietly to the exits. There's no need to panic and DON'T RUN.'

Weeeeeeeooooooooweeee

Ripley looked down at her friends. What was happening? What should she do?

'Come on,' said Psycho. 'Let's get out of here.'

'What about my…' Rip started.

'Rip, get down here! You're not doin' your stupid speech now!' yelled JP.

'Leave her,' said Taz. 'Let her get roasted alive.'

'Roasted?' said Rip. 'But I don't smell a fire, do you?'

'It's the fire alarm,' said JP. 'Must be a fire.'

'All I can smell is lemon,' said Rip.

'What?' said Taz, who instantly stopped walking towards the exit.

eooooooweeeeooooo!

'She's right,' said Psycho, sniffing the air. 'It's lemon. Lemon and bleach.'

The four looked at each other. Three of them knew, all too well, what that smell meant. JP frowned then took a deep breath and called out to the empty canteen, 'Scarlett, what have you done now?'

eooooooweeeeooooo!

The other students had now jostled their way out of the two fire exits in opposite corners of the room, but one of the female teachers remained behind.

'Come on, you lot,' said the teacher. 'Out you go to the assembly point.'

The friends looked at each other. Had Scarlett set fire to the school or had she done something else? Something even worse. Something truly terrible. The two police officers they'd seen earlier ran in, followed by a fireman, who thundered past them wearing an oversized helmet, fluorescent jacket and heavy boots. They were searching for something. As the teacher ushered JP, Ripley, Taz and Psycho out of the door, they looked back over their shoulders. Psycho filmed the fireman as he knelt down and pulled away the red curtain that hid the legs of the temporary stage on which Ripley had been standing, just moments before. They'd found what they were looking for.

Under the stage were two large gas canisters, a plastic barrel half-filled with some sort of liquid and a lunchbox with coloured wires taped to it. The police officers began to back away and, as the fireman got to his feet and did the same, two javelins and six large kitchen knives plunged from the ceiling and thudded into the stage forming a glinting crown of blades.

Ripley gasped. 'Oh… my… God! She nearly got me, too!'

19

The Black Van

JP, Rip, Taz and Psycho sat on a low wall in the playground and watched the chaotic events unfold. The police had pushed back the evacuated students and staff and put up a cordon around the school. The Bomb Disposal Unit took ages to arrive and, in the meantime, frantic parents began to turn up at the gates. Some had heard the first wild rumours that there'd been a massacre. Seeing visions in their heads of psychotic emo boys spraying their classmates with bullets, they'd broken speed limits or left cars parked in the middle of roads in their desperation to get to the school. One or two even suspected their own antisocial offspring might be the perpetrators and approached the gates with an unbearable feeling of dread. Eventually, all the remaining parents were telephoned, a more accurate story was circulated, and those who'd been unable to get there sooner arrived.

The students swapped rumours, too. The first was about the incident in the teachers' car park. It appeared that it was not a delinquent student who'd broken a windscreen or tried to steal a car, as was originally suspected. Instead, a teacher had noticed that a number of petrol caps were missing and that his own tank was empty, when he knew he'd actually filled up on the way to work that morning. The possibility that there was a criminal on the premises with several gallons of petrol was considered a massive cause for concern and the Headmaster had agreed.

A discreet call was made to the local police. While the search for the fuel thief began, word reached the Headmaster that there had been other break-ins, too. The sports hall store had been smashed open and the kitchen was missing equipment and corrosive cleaning chemicals. Even the physics lab seemed to have been ransacked. As the police and staff compiled a list, the cold hand of fear had grabbed them. Petrol, an electronics tool kit, knives, gas canisters, javelins, drain cleaner, cockroach poison. The list was very worrying indeed.

Ripley felt sick when she heard about the drain cleaner and cockroach poison. 'She was gonna use that next, wasn't she?'

'Wait 'til Forensics test the vegetable pasta and the custard,' said Scarlett, but nobody heard her.

Scarlett was alone on the bus back to Sunshine Street. Most of the pupils had been collected by their traumatised parents and driven home, so Scarlett sat on her favourite seat upstairs, invisible, without her friends and in silence. She breathed on the window, drew a heart with her ghost-finger and stared thoughtfully at the drips as they chased each other down the glass. She'd failed again. Not only failed, but probably lost the four best friendships she'd ever had.

Once, she'd been an ordinary, if odd-looking, teenager, with her whole ordinary life ahead of her, but now she was nothing – a phantom, a cloud of gas, a wisp of smoke. A nobody. A hated nobody. She wasn't going to listen to GrimD any more. All that sneaking about, writing on walls, sprinkling nuts on ice-creams, pushing heaters into pools, poisoning custard – it was all so horrible, so sordid. It wasn't like her to be heartless and cruel like that.

Worst of all, she now felt more alone than ever. Examy and Toxicboy were OK, but they didn't know her. She had wanted to discuss with them all the things that she thought were great about being a ghost, like how the warm prickle of walking through doors feels deliciously different to the stomach-churning tingle of concrete. But she couldn't. She couldn't share the excitement of breaking her personal best time for speed-floating to the graveyard, or confide in them about the thrill she got passing her hand through Psycho's chest and touching his heart. They wouldn't really understand. Only her friends would get it. She didn't have Ripley or Taz to hold back her hair when she ghost-puked. Her ghost-heart ached for all the fun times she'd had making movies with Psycho and JP. She even missed their gentle teasing and the name-calling. How she would love it now if JP shouted, 'You smell like corpses; are you dead, Scarlett?' instead of, 'Stop trying to kill us!' Being dead without real friends was rubbish and a whole stinking heap of *merde*!

She got off the bus, by passing through the window, one stop early and drifted across the park. The mountain of wood that was due to be ceremoniously set alight that weekend was now ten or fifteen feet high. The fifth of November fireworks display had been cancelled the previous year because of rain, so the organisers had constructed a huge blue plastic cover and network of ropes to protect the bonfire. No rain was forecast this year but they'd decided to insure against bad weather anyway. There was a stiff breeze in the park and the field was dark, cold and empty.

Brian and Barbara were standing under the climbing tree, arguing. They were always arguing. The last time Scar had seen them, near the swimming pool, the night she'd tried to electrocute Psycho, they'd been arguing. She'd not been close enough to hear them, but Brian had been shouting something while Barbara had been pulling at the collar of his jumper.

Now that she thought about it, they'd been at the ice rink, too, having what looked like a very heated discussion. Perhaps they were like Scarlett and Milton, with that brother-and-sister kinda love-hate relationship thing.

'Oww, you dingleberry! Get out of my way!' Barbara pushed Brian in the chest.

'Dingleberry yourself!' He pushed her back.

'Don't, you'll spoil everything!'

'I shan't spoil anything. Why don't you just mind your own bees' wax?'

Scarlett laughed. She didn't often find it amusing to watch people fight, but these two had a really funny way of talking – sort of old-fashioned, like in kids' telly from years ago, when it was black-and-white instead of colour. Who would actually call someone a *dingleberry*, Scarlett wondered.

Brian suddenly stood still. He had his back to Scarlett so she couldn't see his face, and she wasn't sure why he'd stopped tussling with his sister. Then Barbara rammed her fist into his stomach and he fell backwards, sitting down hard on the damp grass.

Ow, that's gotta hurt, thought Scarlett, scrunching up her face and turning away. When she looked back, Brian was back on his feet but hunched over, while Barbara had climbed into the tree. She must be a brilliant climber, Scarlett thought, because she'd got up there in about a nanosecond! She made a 'V' sign at her brother and he stuck out his tongue. Brian was yummy, especially when he smiled, and Barbara was really funny and would make a brilliant best mate. Scarlett wished they could see her. It would have been be SO cool to have them as friends!

She sighed and headed down the path towards home. There must be a better way than cold-blooded murder to make a cute boy or a cool girl into a ghost like her. There MUST be.

She decided to do a detour past the twins' house at the end of Moonlight Street. Unlike most of their neighbours, Brian and Barbara's house was in darkness. Nobody was home. Perhaps their parents were still out at work, Scarlett thought. As she hovered, suspended in the air above their front garden, a dark green people-carrier rumbled down the road, turned into the drive and stopped. A family got out. There was a mum, a dad, a gran and four children, and none of them looked anything like Brian or Barbara. Scarlett was confused. She looked around her at the rest of the street. Perhaps she'd got the wrong place and Milton had meant another black and white house. But, like Sunshine Street, all the houses were slightly different and this was the only black and white house. Could the twins be living *with* this family? It was a large house, almost the size of Uncle Oswald's, so perhaps that was the answer. Scarlett frowned and floated down an alley, through a couple of gardens and back into Sunshine Street. She would ask Milton when she got home.

There was a van parked in Sunshine Street that she hadn't

seen there before. None of their neighbours owned a black van and it didn't seem to be delivering anything. It had no names or logos painted on the side and there were two men sitting inside, in the dark. Very suspicious! Scarlett pushed her ghost-body through the side of the van. Materialising through metal felt quite nice in a sort of disturbing way, like the sensation of fizzy water all over her skin. It was even darker inside and she couldn't see what was in the back. All she could make out in the street-lamp light coming through the windscreen were the two sinister silhouettes.

'Can I put the heater on?' said the very large, left-hand silhouette.

'Shut up!' said the smaller shape on the right.

'But I'm cold.'

'Shut your girly pie-hole. Should've worn a jumper, like I said.'

'What about the radio then? I'd keep the volume right down,' pleaded the left-hand silhouette.

'No lights, no heater, no kebabs, no burgers, no cup o' tea, no playin' I-spy, and no soddin' radio!' said Mr Right.

Mr Left shifted in his seat and the van wobbled. 'And stop bleedin' fidgeting or I'll stick my hand down your froat and pull ya guts aaat!'

Scarlett had guessed who they were as soon as they'd opened their mouths. It was Simon Bunting's henchmen, the brothers from the other night. They were back and they were 'casing the joint'. This was not a good development. What if they saw Scarlett's friends going into the house? What if they worked out who the monster had been? What if they broke in again tonight, before anyone was ready for them? She didn't really want her friends to be the brothers' next victims, even if they might have succeeded where she had failed. They wouldn't die quickly. The brothers would probably have a bit of fun with their knives and sharpened power tools first. It would be disgusting and probably extraordinarily painful. Scarlett had to get rid of them.

CLICK… 'Oooooh, I love you, baby!' The howl of a sloppy love song poured out of the van's speakers. The brothers both jumped in their seats. The dashboard was lit up like Christmas.

'Hey! I said no radio!' yelled Vladimir. 'Turn it off!'

'I didn't do nuffin,' said Ivan. He fumbled with the radio buttons and only succeeded in changing the station. A rock track blasted out. Vladimir, losing patience with his brother's efforts to find the volume knob, reached for the ignition key and turned it towards him. All the lights went out, the van was silent again and the brothers huffed a sigh of relief.

I must have caught it with my knee, thought Vladimir, embarrassed and annoyed with himself. How could he have been so clumsy, especially after telling his brother all that stuff about keeping quiet?

Then the lights blinked on again and the music blasted.

'*Shake your sexy bootie…*'

'Woah! What's goin'on?' Vlad shouted, as the ignition key turned all the way around and the van's engine spluttered into life. There was another click and the headlights threw their full beams on the front wall of Uncle Oswald's house, where the gang of little kids was moving wheelie bins again.

'Watch out! It's the fuzz!' the kids yelled, then leaped off the bins and ran, terrified, down the street.

'Vlad, the cops!' said Ivan in a panic.

'I heard. Let's get out of here.'

Vladimir slammed the van into gear, released the handbrake and punched his foot on the throttle pedal. The van squealed, in an arc, away from the pavement and Vlad wrenched the gear stick back into reverse; the tyres left a black double 'm' shape on the tarmac as it bounced off the curb then pelted down Sunshine Street like a shiny black bullet.

Scarlett had been thrown out of the van by the first swerve and dumped into the middle of the road. Then she'd experienced a brand new ghost-sensation. She was sitting in the road when the van made its final dash down Sunshine Street and it hit her. The wide mouth of the chrome grill and the massive rubber bumper smashed into her, head-on, at thirty miles per hour. She didn't have time to move or think. The van headed straight for her and, instead of passing through, went SPLAT!

She was jam!

So that's what it feels like, she thought, scraping her bloody, gloopy, jelly-self back into a Scarlett shape again. Pretty cool!

20

The Haunting

'Really, we don't mind them using the cellar,' said Scarlett's dad.

'So long as zey don't 'ave parties or raves or make an 'orrible mess,' said Scarlett's mum.

'Better not touch my collection,' said Scarlett's brother, picking at a large, oozing scab on his knee.

'But you don't understand,' said Scarlett, exasperated. 'I don't mean Rip and Jake and the others.'

'No?' Amandine was wafting around the kitchen, absent-mindedly opening and closing the fridge and cupboard doors.

'No. I'm talking about other people. It was you that warned me in the first place, remember? You said there might be someone out there who'd seen the videos or just spotted this empty house and… you know.'

'You know what, Scar?' said Dad. 'What are you twittering on about?'

Scarlett gritted her teeth and growled. Grrrrrr! Her family were so stupid! How could they be so oblivious to the dangers of modern life and crime and everything?

'THERE COULD BE SQUATTERS AND RAPISTS AND ARSONISTS AND BURGLARS AND TERRORISTS WAITING OUTSIDE TO BREAK IN WHEN NOBODY'S LOOKING, YOU POXY MORONS!' she shouted.

'Scarlett, don't be so melodramatic and don't swear at your mum,' said Dad.

'I said "poxy",' said Scar.

'I don't care. There are hundreds of beautiful words in the English language and you should choose them with a little more consideration, even when you're angry.'

'God, you lot are such festering, rot-brained, drivelling dead lunatics!'

'Ha, well done. Great insult!' said Dad.

Scarlett growled again then realised exactly what would wake them up. 'What if somebody broke in and took your computer?'

Dad's smile sank into a frown.

'With all the stuff you've been writing on it.' Scarlett turned to her mum. 'And your sketchbooks or pens or your box of coloured inks?'

'Why would zay do zat?' Mum asked, her face frozen in horror. Scarlett had hit the bull's-eye.

'Or valuable things you keep in the safe,' Scarlett continued, staring at her brother.

'Anyone touches my samples and I'll stab 'em,' yelled Milton, angrily. 'I'll rip out their guts and stick a fork up their nose and hook their brains out, then I'll wrap their intestines around their necks and hang them up and take their eyeballs and stuff them up their—'

'Yes, thanks, Milton! Very descriptive!' said Dad.

'Yeah, thanks, Milton,' said Scarlett. 'That's exactly what we should all be saying. We've got to prevent the wrong people coming into our house.'

'Mmm,' said Dad. 'Suppose you've got a point.'

'Unless it's completely escaped your notice, we're putrid, lifeless ghosts! Isn't it about time we did some serious haunting?'

http://scardeparted.blogspot.com

Scar Dedd's Haunting Blog – how we plan to avert the painful death of my friends at the hands of evil criminals.

So here I am, blogging again. And I've decided to avoid Ghoolkool for a while. I think they were becoming a bad influence. You see, I've realised that I should have been trying to find ways to communicate with my friends, not ways to exterminate them. What was I thinking?!!

I'm kinda talking a lot more to my family now, too. I still think they're totally bonkers – there's no doubt of that – but I guess Milton's quite funny and Mum and Dad aren't so bad, as 'rents go. They've had some great ideas for the... No, I'll tell you all about that later. Don't want to spoil the surprise.

The friends sat in the cellar on Saturday afternoon and JP went through the final preparations for their performance: the brilliant effects that would scare the burglars away forever and let them keep the basement as their winter HQ. They'd been at the Dedds' house all day Friday, too, because the school had been closed while the canteen was still a crime scene.

Taz couldn't stop fidgeting. '*Everyone* will be at the firework display,' she grumbled.

'Which is exactly why we shouldn't be.' JP had tried to convince Taz that tonight would be the perfect opportunity for the intruders to return. 'If everyone is in the park, watching fireworks, then nobody will be in the street.'

'You don't want to have to go back to that bench in the park, do you?' said Rip.

Taz still desperately wanted to go to the bonfire party. She'd heard Max Rocket was going to be there and he was a *dream god*. 'Can't I go to the party first and meet you later?' she suggested.

JP shook his head. 'We all gotta be here early – won't work otherwise.'

'You're in charge of phase one,' said Psycho looking up from his laptop.

'I thought *I* was phase one,' said Ripley, who was curled up on the crusty sofa, looking at JP's plans and diagrams.

'You're phase four,' said JP, angrily. 'We'll only have one chance and it's got to be perfect.'

'JP's right,' said Psycho. 'This is gonna be our best project yet. It'll be spectacular!'

By nightfall, everything had been rehearsed and was checked and ready. The friends waited in the dark house. Was JP right? Would tonight be when the intruders would return?

A steady stream of people, wrapped up warmly, trudged along Sunshine Street towards the park and the bonfire party. Their scarf-muffled voices echoed between the houses and filled the frosty evening air with excited laughter.

'Did you know that "laughter" with an "s" in front of it spells "slaughter"?' said Psycho.

'Shhhh,' hissed Ripley.

'You know, Scarlett probably hasn't given up trying to kill us yet.'

'Shut up!' said Taz, with a shiver. 'I don't believe it *was* her, anyway.'

'She might even do something tonight,' Psycho continued. 'A snooker cue through the head... A kitchen knife in the back... A chainsaw...'

JP laughed. 'Yeah. She's gonna slice you up, Taz!'

'Stop it!' Taz wasn't amused. 'You two are evil scumbags!'

'Even now, she could be getting into a lorry,' said JP, 'starting the engine, letting off the handbrake and driving it through the front door to squash us flat like pizza!'

'Jay, shut your stupid face!' yelled Ripley. 'I can hear something.'

They listened. There was another sound outside, mingling with the laughter: a diesel engine rattle. A vehicle was approaching.

'Told you,' said Psycho. 'It's Scarlett and she's going to drive backwards and forwards over your corpse until it's *Taz soup!*'

The rattle stopped.

Outside, Ivan and Vladimir's van had done a three-point turn at the gate, then parked facing the way it had come, ready for a quick getaway. The van was still.

Eventually, the last stragglers entered the park and the street was quiet again. Quiet as the grave. The doors of the van opened and two dark figures emerged. They crept to the back of the vehicle, lifted out a heavy bag, then headed silently towards the house. At the gate, the smaller figure stopped and looked furtively over his shoulder. There was no sign of the wheelie-bin kids, nor any meddling Sunshine Street residents. The gate gave a tiny, frightened squeak as they pushed it open and the two menacing figures disappeared into the thick shadow of the house.

Wooooooooooooooooooo.

'Whassat?' said Ivan. He'd heard a faint moan, like wind whistling through floorboards.

'S'nuffin,' said Vladimir.

'You sure there's nobody here?'

'I told you. It's empty.'

'And the monster was…'

'Just a loada kids muckin' about, like I said. They'll be in the park tonight.'

'Just kids… just kids,' Ivan muttered to himself and crawled through the kitchen window, which his brother had just levered open with a crowbar.

This time they headed straight for the cellar. They'd brought all the tools they needed to open the safe.

'Right,' said Vladimir, resting his torch on the arm of the sofa so that it illuminated the solid grey door of the Pottinger 340. 'Hand me the drill first.'

Ivan put down his own torch and began to take all the heavy equipment out of the bag and lay it out neatly on the snooker table. There was another crowbar, some pliers, wire-cutters, screwdrivers, a couple of hammers, a pair of goggles, a chisel, a box of heavy-duty drill bits, a cordless drill, detonators, a slab of plastic explosive, a baseball bat, a large knife and a gun.

'Hurry up. We're not 'avin' a bleedin' dinner party,' said Vladimir.

'Here,' said Ivan, wiping some dried blood off a drill bit, slotting it into the cordless drill and handing it to his brother.

Woooooooooooooooooo.

'There's that sound again,' said Ivan.

'It's the wind,' said Vladimir. 'Goggles.' He held out his hand and Ivan gave him the goggles. 'What time is it?'

Ivan looked at his watch. 'Um… big hand is on the… little hand is… It's half past seven.'

'Perfect,' said Vladimir.

'What is?' Ivan asked, then jumped like he'd touched a live wire as a flash of light exploded through a tiny high window and lit up the whole cellar. It was followed by a huge BANG! The firework display had started. Ivan put his fingers in his ears and his brother began to drill. Ivan went over to the high window to watch the pretty flares and flashes. The glass was very dirty and hadn't been cleaned for years, but he could still see the glittering fountains of red and green and white and blue. The room went dark again for a moment and Ivan looked at his brother, who'd stopped drilling.

They waited.

Ivan turned back to the grimy window but, out of the corner of his eye, he caught sight of something blinking. A red light. He stared at it. How strange. A tiny red light hovered above him in the inky darkness. He was about to open his mouth and tell Vlad about it when the whoosh of another rocket drew his gaze back to the window.

The crowd in the park whooped and cheered as the spectacular pyrotechnics reached a deafening climax. Vladimir had almost finished, too. He put down the drill and reached for a chisel and hammer.

'Just a little tap here,' he said, ramming the chisel blade into the lock mechanism. 'And we're sorted.' He brought the hammer down with a crunch. There was a final huge volley of explosions in the park followed by applause, cheers and shouts, then the safe door made a hollow *THUNK* sound.

Ivan jumped excitedly across the room. 'You did it!'

Vladimir grabbed the handle, pushed it down and pulled the door towards him. The rusty hinges groaned and the door rasped open.

Scarlett's ghost-brother, Milton, had been waiting for what felt like hours, hunched inside the safe and, as the pair of burglars peered into the gloom, he leaped up. He had adorned his invisible ghost-boy body with his putrid collection. An evil-smelling, festering mass of mashed worms, wasp corpses, rat tails, egg shells, frog spawn, pond slime, cat poo, rotten apple skins, spider webs, drain gloop and mouldy cheese sprang at the henchmen, with a stomach-churning squelch.

'Aaaaaaaaaaaahhhhhhhhhhhh!'

Ivan and Vladimir staggered backwards and slammed into the snooker table.

The collection hit them both right in the face.

SPLAT! 'Eeeeerrrrrrrr!

Ivan clawed at a piece of writhing, maggoty cheese that had gone up his nose and into his mouth, while Vladimir tried to scrape a lump of sticky, foul-smelling cat poo out of his hair.

They began to retch and heave.

'I think I'm gonna be...' Ivan spat out a dead wasp and staggered towards the stairs holding his stomach.

'What's going on?' yelled Vladimir.

He was coughing and trying not to throw up his tea. He grabbed the baseball bat and his torch and swept the beam around the room.

'Who's there? Izzit you bloody kids again?'

He shone the torch into the safe.

Apart from the pungent remains of Milton's collection dripping from the shelves the safe was empty.

There was no cash. No jewellery. Nothing.

He swore loudly and slammed the door then stuffed the large knife and the gun into his pockets, picked up the torch and the baseball bat and followed his brother out of the cellar.

JP, Rip, Taz and Psycho were waiting for them in the hall.

Woooooooo!

A glowing, flapping white shape sailed down the stairs towards the brothers.

'Wooooooo!' Taz moaned into a microphone from her hiding place under the hall table and an unsettling, distorted sound echoed through the house. She pulled on the rope and the white shape shivered and floated upwards again.

'G-g-ghosts!' screamed Ivan.

'S'not. It's bleedin' kids!' yelled Vladimir and waved the baseball bat in the air.

JP, who was hiding behind the living-room door, saw the bat and gulped. Time for phase two. He flicked the two switches in his hand and the dry-ice machine hidden in the kitchen began to fill the hall with an eerie mist. A mist that was pulsing with green light.

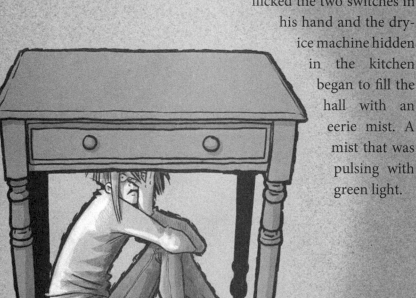

Ivan whimpered but his brother wasn't going to be scared so easily. 'They'll have to do better than that,' he said, laughing.

Psycho was crouching halfway up the stairs, holding his video camera in one hand and the remote control for phase three in the other. He pressed a button on the remote and the data projector threw an image on to the green cloud, one of his best-ever movie effects. He'd created it on his computer. The animated monster – part dinosaur, part alien, part Psycho's weird imagination – emerged out of the mist, snarling.

Vladimir emitted a snort of disdain and handed the baseball bat to Ivan. Then he reached for the knife in his pocket and drew out the long, razor-sharp blade. It glistened in the green light. Ripley, who was crouching above him on the first floor, behind the banisters, saw the knife glinting in his hand and stifled a scream. Help! It wasn't going the way they'd planned it at all. Phase four, phase four! She reached up and tipped all of the four buckets balanced on the handrail and about twenty litres of fake blood rained down on Ivan and Vladimir.

SPLOOOSSSHHH!

A sticky, red puddle of syrup and food dye spread like a gory lake across the black and white tiles. The brothers wiped their eyes and looked up at the swinging buckets.

JP, Rip, Taz and Psycho peeked from their hiding places. What had they been thinking? How did they ever imagine that they could frighten off these seriously scary burglars with their pathetic, amateur horror effects? Now the men looked angrier and more terrifying than ever. Two mean-looking blokes, soaked in blood, white eyes staring, waving knives and baseball bats! The four of them were going to be murdered for sure!

JP imagined the headlines:

TEENS MASSACRED IN BONFIRE-NIGHT BLOODBATH

He hoped he'd die quickly. A sliced jugular vein and rapid blood loss, before peaceful oblivion.

Taz thought about how angry her parents were going to be. They'd only just bought her a new flute and now she was going to get her body chopped up into small pieces and buried in a shallow grave.

Ripley was furious. She'd have her head smashed into a pulp by a baseball bat and that worm, Max Rocket, who'd still have an intact head, would be School President. It was so unfair!

Only Psycho wasn't thinking about a painful death at the hands of the thugs. He was distracted by something. He was staring at the puddle of fake blood, which had started to ripple and heave.

The Dedds Get Serious

'If you kids tell us where you hid the money, we'll forget all about this,' said Vladimir. 'Right, Ivan?'

'Right,' Ivan agreed. 'We won't hurt you. We promise.'

Ripley thought Ivan's voice sounded really sinister, like the cannibalistic serial killer in a very gory movie they'd watched once at Psycho's house. She trembled.

'Look, I'm putting my knife away… and my bruvver's gonna put down the bat.' Vladimir eased the blade of the knife into the back of his trousers and Ivan placed the bat on the hall table, right above Taz's head. The men held out their dripping red hands to prove they were empty, but Taz saw Vladimir reaching into his pocket again. He must have another weapon, she thought. This is bad – really bad! She hoped her friends wouldn't fall for the trick and come out of their hiding places. If they could all keep quiet and stay still, perhaps the thugs would get bored and just go away.

Taz didn't have to worry about Psycho. He definitely wasn't falling for it. He wasn't even listening. He was puzzled and becoming increasingly fearful, watching the floor. Something was growing. Strange shapes were bulging up out of the red syrup. Two pulsating columns of fake blood.

'What the f…?' Ivan and Vladimir had noticed them, too. The columns were growing limbs… with claw-like hands… and sharp, flesh-tearing fingers… and heads… with waving, writhing hair… and deep black cavernous eye sockets… and gaping mouths full of dripping red teeth! The blood-drenched figures loomed over the brothers, leaned forward, opened their terrifying mouths and spewed a torrent of gore into their faces.

'Aaaaaaaaaagggggghhhh!' The brothers screamed now in genuine terror. This wasn't kids – it was too realistic.

Vladimir pulled the gun out of his sticky pocket and waved it at the taller bloody shape but, before he could pull the trigger, it was wrenched from his hand and thrown across the hallway, spraying a gash of crimson droplets up the wall. Ivan was trying to run but the syrup puddle sucked at his boots and forced him into a slow-motion lurch towards the front door. He reached out, turned the handle and opened it enough to taste the cool air of freedom, then *SLAM!* An invisible hand rammed it shut again. The brothers looked at each other in panic, then over at the kitchen door. The kitchen window was still open! They lifted their gloopy feet and squelched in an hysterical dash around the monsters and across the puddle.

'LET'S GET OUT OF HERE!' screamed Vladimir, his mouth filling with the fake gore.

But the kitchen door slammed, too. Vladimir rattled the handle and pushed. Someone was pushing from the other side. He glanced over his shoulder. There were three more doors. Where did they lead? Could there be another way out? Vlad remembered the knife and reached behind his back. Now smeared with blood, the blade looked even more terrifying. Vlad looked at Ivan and then nodded towards the door to the conservatory. He thrust the knife out in front and they charged at the door, but skidded to a halt as they came face-to-face with the blood-monsters again, hideous mouths opened, ready to drench them with red spew once more. Vladimir looked down at his arm. The knife had gone *through* the glistening red fiend, right up to his elbow.

'Aaaaaaarrrrggghhhh!'

Vlad and Ivan took a step back, tripped and fell. They'd fallen over something and now found themselves sitting in the middle of the puddle. The *something* writhed and curled in the revolting, sticky lake. It seemed to unfurl an endless, thrashing, red limb, which sprang in the air and looped itself around the now-petrified brothers. The dripping rope wound itself tighter and tighter, until Vladimir and Ivan were helpless. They couldn't move.

'Mmnnnn,' Ivan whimpered.

'What's that smell?' moaned Vladimir.

'Lemons?'

'No, I think I messed my pants.'

'Vlad? D'you see that?' Ivan tried to point but couldn't lift his arm.

'The bloody writing on the wall, you mean?' said Vlad.

'Yeah.'

They looked up at the wall, halfway up the staircase, where they could see three sickening words had been daubed in the viscous red syrup.

Below the words there now stood four hideous figures, saturated in the glistening crimson gore. The gruesome quartet gripped the handrail with red claws, their ghastly mouths grinned and eight deep, black, cavernous eyes stared down at the now-powerless henchmen.

'OK, OK, we confess!'

'We've 'urt people…'

'We done blackmail, torture, freats.'

'For our boss.'

'For Mr Buntin'.'

'We freatened Oswald Dedd… and blackmailed 'im.'

'And stole all his money!'

'We stole lots of people's money.'

'We confess!'

'Yeah, wc confess.'

'We're crooks and we 'urt people.'

'Not killers!'

'No, we never murdered no one.'

'But we did steal stuff.'

'And we're really, really sorry.'

'Please don't hurt me. It was Vlad's idea.'

Blue lights were flashing outside. There were sirens and the sound of running boots thundering towards the house. A fist hammered on the door.

'Open up! Police! Open the door! Who's in there?'

Scarlett, still covered in fake blood, floated to the front door and opened it. Two uniformed police officers tumbled into the hallway. They'd been about to break the door down with a heavy battering ram. They regained their balance and shone torches into the gloom.

'Police! What's going on?' said the taller PC.

The shorter one spotted Vlad and Ivan and gagged. 'Oh cripes! Call an ambulance!'

'Thank God you're here!' cried Vladimir, tears rolling down his face.

JP, Rip, Taz and Psycho sat in the back of an ambulance. What had just happened? How had their horror effects disaster suddenly become a *real haunting*? They were impressed. That last bit – those bloody creatures… How had Scarlett done it? How did she create all that amazing stuff? She was awesome.

They watched as Vladimir and Ivan were bundled into the back of a police car, their skin and clothes stained red by the fake blood. It had taken ages to convince the confused paramedics that nobody was injured.

'It's not real,' Ripley had pleaded.

'Really, we don't need stitches or a drip,' said Taz.

'Taste it,' said JP. 'It's syrup.'

'We wondered why we couldn't find any wounds,' said the first medic.

'How did you manage to disarm them and tie them up?' asked the second medic.

'It wasn't us, it was…' Taz began. Rip kicked her.

Psycho pointed his camera out of the ambulance and zoomed in on a police car, which had its doors open. One of the wheelie-bin kids was sitting in the back seat, being questioned by a policeman. The kid pointed at the ambulance, then the policeman walked towards them. Psycho groaned.

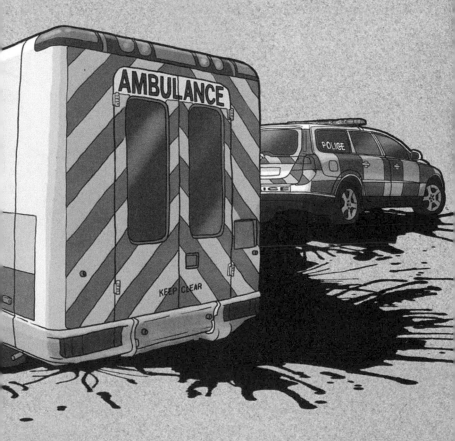

Wolfgang, Amandine, Scarlett and Milton had retreated upstairs after the police arrived. They'd floated up through the house and out of the attic on to the roof. They were still a little sticky with a revolting mixture of ghost-puke and fake gore, and slightly visible, so didn't want to be discovered by the police forensic team. What a shock that would be!

'Wow! That was incredible!' said Scarlett, standing on the ridge tiles and throwing her arms wide with delight. She was worn out but elated.

'Eet was fan-tas-tique!' said Mum, beaming.

'Brilliant! Just brilliant! How did you and Dad do that gushing-blood thing? You were completely awesome!'

'Just popped into our heads, I guess,' said Dad.

'And what did you do to them in the cellar, Milt?' she turned to her brother. 'They were wetting themselves.'

'Sacrificed my collection but it was worth it,' said Milton, brushing a large clot of gore-vomit off his sweatshirt, then climbing on to the chimney stack and balancing on one leg.

Scarlett looked down at the park. The embers of the enormous fire were still glowing. There were small clusters of waving torches and sparklers, but most of the fireworks-party crowd had migrated into Sunshine Street. They were huddled behind the police barriers, craning their necks to see what was going on. Their conversations drifted upwards to the roof.

'Lots of blood?'

'Whose blood?'

'Is somebody dead?'

'I thought the Dedds were already dead.'

'What's that weird lemon-bleach smell?'

A taxi was coming down Sunshine Street. It got halfway down the crowded street and had to stop. After a moment, a slightly overweight and awkward man climbed out, stood at the window to pay the driver, then began to push his way through the crowd. He had a mop of curly hair and a hunched way of walking that looked familiar.

Scarlett watched him for a few seconds but was soon distracted. She'd just spotted Brian and Barbara at the edge of the crowd. They were standing alone, a little way back, not arguing but watching what was going on, like the rest of the crowd. Suddenly, the twins glanced upwards at the roof and seemed to look directly at her, like they knew the Dedds' were there. That's creepy, she thought.

'I'm gonna need all your footage,' the policeman

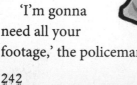

242

said, sternly. Psycho switched off the camera and handed it over. The policeman put it in a plastic evidence bag.

'There are more in the house,' said Psycho. 'In the cellar, the hall and the kitchen.'

'We've got those.'

'Um, Officer?' said JP.

'Sergeant,' said the policeman.

'Sergeant. H-how did you... I mean, who called nine-nine-nine?'

The Sergeant nodded at the kid in the car. 'His gang heard the commotion, thought you lot were in trouble and got on their mobiles.' The cop smiled. 'That boy thinks you're a hero.'

'He does?' said JP.

'Yup. You were on telly, weren't you? That *Fakers* show?'

JP thrust out his chest with pride.

'They've been watching you – knew you were planning something.'

'Ehem!' A chubby, curly-haired man, who'd appeared behind the Sergeant, coughed. 'Excuse me,' said the man, scratching nervously at his head.

'Sorry, sir,' said the Sergeant. 'I'm gonna have to ask you to move back behind the cordon.'

JP, Ripley, Taz and Psycho stared at the man. Had they seen him somewhere before?

'You don't understand,' said the man. 'I have a right to know what's going on. This is my house.'

'Your house?'

'Yes. I'm Dedd.'

'Pardon?'

'Oswald Dedd.'

Scarlett watched the henchmen being driven away. Then her friends' worried parents arrived and they all went off to the police station, too. She watched them as they headed down Sunshine Street and turned the corner. She was glad they were OK. She would have felt terrible if anything disgusting or painful had happened to them.

A flash was followed by a clap of thunder rumbling in the distance and a few wet spots landed on the roof tiles. It was going to rain after all. The drops got bigger and the thunder rumbled again. Slowly, a dark cloud drifted until it was hanging over the house, then released a torrent. The Dedds laughed and began to dance together in a sort of celebration. The rain washed off all the fake blood, which ran down the roof, into the gutters and away down the drain.

http://scardeparted.blogspot.com

Scar Dedd's Haunting Blog – how we succeeded in averting the painful deaths of my friends at the hands of evil criminals.

Woo-hoo! WE DID IT! The Dedds were A-MAZE-ING!

I was REALLY scared for a bit, like when the little bloke brought out A GUN, but Milt was the one who got it off him. He'd seen a disarmament technique in an SAS computer game, or something. Anyway. I tied them up – kinda ran around them holding on to the rope from Ripley's rubbish ghost – and when they saw the message Dad had written on the wall it was priceless! PRICELESS! Dad spent hours writing and rewriting that line.

Give yourselves up...

Confess the Truth...

Get out or face the consequences... (that one had just been too long for the wall).

22

Tea with Oswald

'You knock,' said Psycho, pushing JP forward.

'Why do I have to do it?' said JP.

'You're pathetic,' said Ripley and she jumped up the steps. 'We've got to warn him that his house is haunted.' She knocked three times on the Dedds' front door, then stepped back down to stand with the others.

They waited.

And waited.

Ripley was about to try again when they heard footsteps. The door opened and Oswald Dedd frowned at them.

'H-hello,' said Rip. 'We're…'

Oswald flipped his glasses down from the top of his head to rest on his nose. He peered at them. 'Oh, yes,' he said. His face broke into a smile. 'You're Scarlett's friends.'

The friends looked at each other. How did he know that?

'Come in, come in,' said Oswald. He opened the door wide and disappeared across the hallway, which was a lot cleaner than the last time they'd seen it. Ripley led the way up the steps and they all followed Oswald into the kitchen. 'Tea?' he asked.

'Yes, please.'

'Cake or Jammy Dodgers? They're a type of biscuit. My brother and I used to call them Dodgy Jammers.' He stared out of the window then smiled and flicked the switch on the kettle.

They had prepared an explanation of what they had been doing in the house and how sorry they were. They also wanted to thank him for deciding not to press charges.

'We're really sorry about your brother's family,' said Ripley, in her best, empathetic-politician voice. 'You must have been very sad when you found out.'

'Mm,' said Oswald, not sounding very sad at all. He was getting cups and a teapot out of a cupboard.

'We went to the funeral. It was… nice,' said Taz. Ripley glared at her and she glared back. What was she supposed to say?

'We wanted to say sorry,' said JP. 'For breaking in and everything. We knew the house was empty and we only used the cellar because it was cold outside.'

'And we'll pay for any damage,' said Psycho, without thinking, and he instantly regretted it. Had there been a lot of expensive damage for which he'd just claimed responsibility?

Oswald was looking for something in the back of the fridge. 'I'm sure I've got some butter somewhere,' he mumbled. 'We could have buttered toast. I love buttered toast with a cup of tea. Don't you?'

'Was there a lot of mess?' Taz asked, remembering the spotless floor they'd just walked across in the hallway.

'I got a cleaner in,' said Oswald, waving four slices of bread at them, then putting them in the toaster.

'We made statements to the police about those gangsters,' JP explained.

'I never got my cameras back though,' said Psycho.

'Ooo, yes! Your cameras!' Oswald ran out of the room.

The friends stared at each other. Scarlett's uncle was mental. He wasn't acting as they'd expected and he was making it really hard to apologise. Oswald came back and dropped several plastic-wrapped packages on to the table.

'Your cameras. The police copied the memory cards, of course. The projector and your dry-ice machine are outside. Bit heavy to carry.'

'Great – thanks!' said Psycho. 'So my videos are evidence then?'

'Yeah, but apparently, so my solicitor says, apart from the confession, there's not much to see. The police are so excited about catching Ivan and Vladimir red-handed, so to speak, they don't seem to care about your *haunting*.' He chuckled. 'Red-handed! He he he! I hear their confession was magnificent.'

'Are you gonna have to go to court?' said JP.

'Yup. I won't be alone, though. Lots of their victims have come forward. They're all giving evidence. Those boys'll go to prison for a long time. Not sure there's enough to get their boss, yet – just the brothers' word, at the moment, and they're hardly the best witnesses, but…'

'So it's true; we stopped a major crime gang, not just burglars?' said Rip.

'And *you're* not really a crim, are you?' said Taz.

'I know what everyone's been thinking. I'm a coward and should have told the police about the threats, right at the beginning, instead of running away. And my stupidity might have put my brother's family in danger. But, I really didn't think Ivan and Vladimir knew where I lived or were stupid enough to think I'd have any money here. But, hey, nobody got hurt. They were dead already, right?'

'Why did you come home then?' asked Taz, shocked at his cheerful explanation.

'I thought about it every day, but, well, when I saw in an article in a newspaper that they had all died, I felt really bad. It was time to face the music,' he said with a grin.

Ripley frowned. Oswald's attitude to their mass poisoning was a bit cold. He was either completely heartless or stupid. Even so, she had to tell him. How could she find a way to break it to him that everything wasn't all right? 'We got you a card,' she said, taking a yellow envelope out of her bag. The card had a picture of a sunflower on it and inside they'd written,

Dear Mr Dedd
sorry your family is dead
sorry we messed up your hous
thank you for not making us
go to jail
love from
Ripley JP Psycho Taz.

Oswald laughed when he read it. 'Thanks, kids. There was no way I was going to press charges, you know. Wasn't that night enough of a scare for you?'

Ripley was starting to get a bit annoyed. Why was Oswald Dedd laughing at them? They had tried to be mature and polite, coming to apologise – offer their condolences. And he was talking about Scarlett and her family as if he thought their deaths were an hilarious joke. He wasn't normal.

'You can stop worrying, you know,' said Oswald, still laughing. 'Scarlett told me all about you.'

'What?'

'Did you think I wouldn't find out the family is, y'know… still here?'

'The family?' They were stunned. Since the events of bonfire night, they'd suspected that Scarlett might not be the only ghost in the house. They weren't certain, but it did seem to be the only explanation for the awesome haunting, even if it was pretty mind blowing. How had Oswald found out?

'Was quite a shock, of course.' He laughed again. 'Scarlett wrote me a note in the steam on my bathroom mirror. I thought I was losing my marbles.'

'What did the note say?' Taz interrupted. Ripley scowled at her again. 'Don't look at me like that, Rip. You wanted to ask, too.'

'Can't remember.' Oswald scratched his head. 'Something like *hello, how are you?*'

'So what did she tell you about us?'

'Come with me,' said Oswald, putting the teapot down on the table and heading for the door again. 'Come on.' They followed him across the hall and into the conservatory.

'How's it going?' said Oswald. The conservatory was empty. Who was he talking to?

Then they heard the tapping. It was coming from the computer on the desk. The same computer that had given them such a fright upstairs on their second visit. Someone was typing. Someone invisible. A ghost.

'They're here, aren't they?' Ripley whispered, scanning the room, nervously.

'My brother, Wolfgang,' said Oswald, pointing at the computer, where the word 'hello' appeared on the screen. 'His wife, Amandine.' They looked at the other side of the desk where Oswald now indicated. A pen was hanging in the air above a sketchbook. It waved at them and went back to scratching a black line across the page. 'Scarlett and Milton are probably in their bedrooms but, just in case they're here, hello kids!' A magazine lifted off the table and flapped, then the chaise longue rocked and creaked, as if someone was sitting on it.

'Oh. My. God! It's really true!' said Taz. 'They're *all* ghosts!'

'They had a bit of trouble getting used to it at the beginning,' said Oswald. 'Apparently, they used to throw up if they tried to get someone's attention. Pretty horrible by all accounts. Scarlett said she wanted to talk to you lot really badly, but she couldn't.'

'She did more than talking,' whispered Ripley. The four friends looked at each other and smiled.

'They're a lot better at it now,' said Oswald. 'They can control their ghost-reflexes. I can't hear them but they write messages all the time. Scarlett's got a blog. You should read it. She mentions all of you.'

'Look,' said Psycho. He'd noticed that something was happening to the windows. Someone was breathing on them. Letters began to appear.

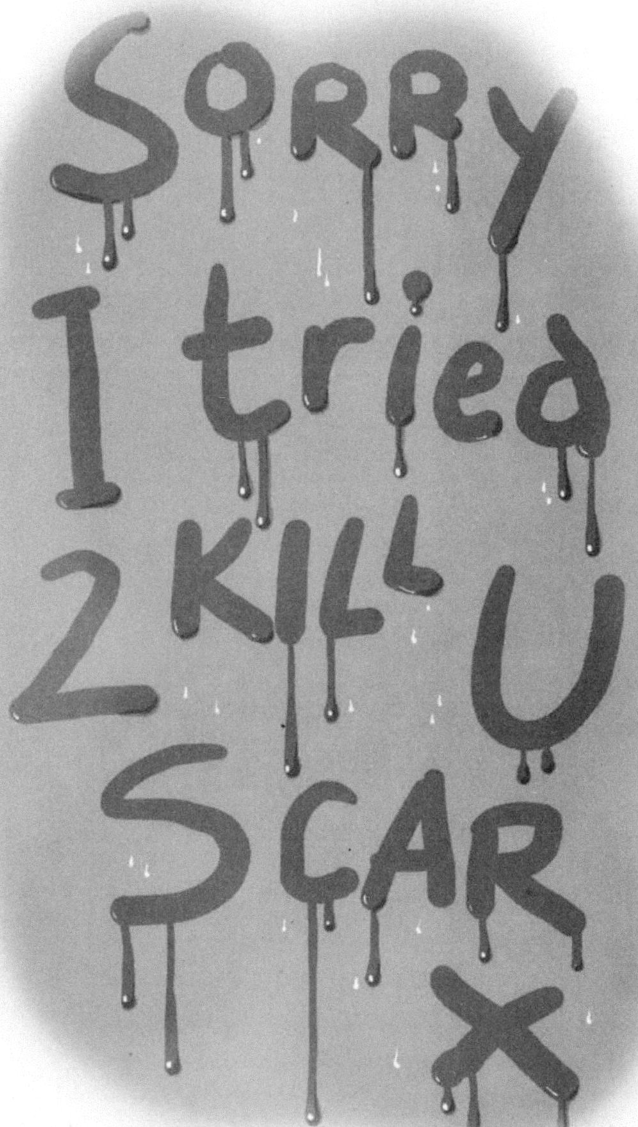
SORRY
I tried
2 KILL U
SCAR
x

23

Wolf & Mandy

'Psycho, it's starting,' Taz yelled. 'Get in here and bring the pizzas.'
She ran back into Oswald Dedd's sitting-room and joined Ripley
and JP on the sofa. JP had his arm around Ripley's shoulder and
was trying to move his hand down to the front of her jumper.

'Is he coming?' asked Rip, swatting his hand away.

'Yeah,' said Taz.

The door opened again and Psycho stumbled into the room,
dropping four steaming cardboard pizza boxes that had just been
delivered on to the coffee table. The show was starting. Oswald
reached for the remote control but it slipped from his grasp and
flew across the room, hanging in mid-air for a moment. An
invisible finger pressed the volume button. They stared at the

screen. It was the pilot episode of a brand new animated show called *Sunshine Street*. The title sequence began.

'Yay!' They all cheered.

The programme ended.

'Excellent!' said JP.

'Superb!' said Psycho.

Oswald opened a bottle of champagne and poured it into five glasses.

'A toast!' he yelled. 'To Wolf and Mandy!'

They lifted their glasses of foam in the air.

'To haunted houses!' said JP.

'To the dead!' said Taz.

'To the Dedd!' they all agreed.

'Who put *mushrooms* on my pizza?' said Psycho, opening a box.

'Psych! That's not funny,' said Taz. 'He's only joking, Scarlett.'

Scarlett slammed the box lid down on Psycho's hand.

Now that you have found this, I hope you go back and read all my earlier posts. I want to explain why I tried to kill you all. I thought it was for, y'know, all the right reasons... It felt right at the time, anyway. There was this boy in a chat room and he was suggesting stuff, manipulating me. It was all pretty freaky and scary. Well, he kind of convinced me that making you dead, too, was the answer to all my, y'know, life-sickness problems. Whateva. Didn't succeed, did I? SO glad I didn't murder you all. And I'll say it again – I am SO SORRY!

So here's my update...

Probably happiest teen-ghost on the planet. Wolf & Mandy books are a complete success overdose. As you probably noticed, they have this raving, cult teen following and have now hit the mainstream bestseller lists, too. So proud of 'rents! They are the coolest dead 'rents in the world. Dad's stories and Mum's pics are the hottest thing in publishing and now there's a rockin' animated TV series. Awesome, right? We don't mind that Uncle Oswald is getting all the credit... and the dosh. He admitted he'd been a rot-brain dung-wit to be suckered by Simon 'Liquidiser' Bunting and his gang, but he's learned his lesson about that gambling malarkey. Anyway, he has bills to pay and a haunted house to run.

Scarlett opened the front door for her friends as they crossed the hallway to go home.

'Thanks, Scar,' said Ripley.

'See you tomorrow,' said Psycho. 'I mean, we won't *see* you tomorrow.'

'Bye, Mr Dedd,' said Taz, giggling. 'Thanks for the champagne.'

'You can all call me Oswald,' said Oswald. 'And don't tell your folks I gave you bubbly!'

'Bye, Oswald! Bye, Dedds!' they shouted at the house.

A group of kids was waiting for them down at the gate. There were always *Wolf & Mandy* fans outside the house these days. Sometimes a few ghost-hunters, too. The Dedds' house was a place of pilgrimage for horror fans. The kids waved posters, plastic figures and copies of *Wolf & Mandy* books.

'Are you friends with the ghosts?'

'What do they look like?'

'You're JP and Psycho, aren't you? I've seen your movies on YouTube.'

'Can I be in your next one?'

'Do you know Wolf and Mandy?'

Scarlett watched JP, Taz, Rip and Psycho sign autographs and pose for photos. Then, as her friends walked down Sunshine Street, arm-in-arm, she drifted out of the house and into the park. It was getting dark. She'd have a last speed-float around the park and head back home for the *haunting*. The fans were expecting a performance and the Dedds didn't want to disappoint them. They'd give them some cool video footage to show their sceptical school mates.

As she whooshed past the climbing tree she noticed the striped socks and turned back. Brian and Barbara were arguing as usual.

'It was your fault!'

'You were driving!'

'You distracted me!'

'What are you looking at?'

'What?' said Scarlett. Brian and Barbara were looking straight at her!

'You're staring!' said Barbara. 'It's impolite to stare… and to listen to other people's conversations.'

'Don't, Bar,' hissed Brian. 'She's not being rude.'

'He's only saying that 'cos he fancies you,' said Barbara, pushing her brother in the chest. Brian pushed her back and she fell out of the tree, landing awkwardly on her head.

Scarlett leaped forward. 'Are you all right?'

Barbara was laughing. 'Of course I'm all right.'

'She's always been clumsy,' said Brian, jumping down beside them, 'which is why the accident was *her fault.*'

'It wasn't!' Barbara looked at Scarlett. 'She's staring again.'

'You can see me!' said Scarlett.

'Brian, your girlfriend is

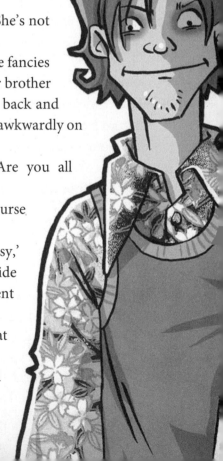

officially rude *and* stupid!' said Barbara.

Brian glared at her.

'But... but... does that mean you're...?' Scarlett was astonished.

'We wanted to talk to you but we both know what it's like, don't we, Bar, in the beginning, when everything is crazy and confusing. So we waited.' Brian smiled reassuringly and Scarlett's stomach flipped over. He was SO cute.

'And now you've found out,' said Barbara. 'You're really slow, y'know. We thought you'd guess ages ago.'

The twins smiled. Scarlett's brain felt all jumbled up, like she'd been shaken upside down. They could see her. They were like her. Were they ghosts, too? But why...?

'Why...?' Scarlett started to ask, then stopped. She was about to ask the really stupid question, 'Why are you dead?' but began to remember all the times she'd seen them in the park, at the ice rink, near the swimming pool. She decided to ask a different question. 'Why... are you always arguing?' she asked instead.

'Go on,' said Barbara, nodding at her brother. 'You tell her what you wanted to do.'

'I wanted to stop you, but Bar wouldn't let me.'

'Stop me what?'

'Trying to kill your friends.'

'We know what GrimD does, you see,' said Barbara.

'GrimD?' Scarlett was even more confused.

'He tried it on us, too. Y'know. "Aren't you lonely? Wouldn't you like your friends to be dead, too?" That perverted grooming he does with the newly dead.'

'So, why didn't you stop me?'

'It's like Brian said,' said Bar. 'When you're a new ghost, things are pretty intense.'

'And also, Grim can get quite possessive,' Brian explained. 'She was right to stop me. It could have been worse. GrimD's been known to get really nasty.'

'You had to learn the hard way, but you're stronger now because of it,' said Barbara. 'Because we left you alone.'

Scarlett was still frowning, still confused. 'You're both ghosts?'

'Yes,' the twins replied.

'You're dead?'

'Yes.' Barbara rolled her eyes impatiently.

'So you died? I mean. How? How did you die?' Scar asked. 'If that's not a rude question.'

They pointed at the tree.

'The climbing tree? Did you fall out of it, or something?'

Barbara snorted. 'Nah, much worse.' She slapped her hand on the trunk. There was a gash in the bark that Scarlett had never noticed before. It looked like it had happened a very long time ago and healed over, like a scab.

'Fifth November, 1973,' said Brian. 'It was a dare. We stole a car and…'

'*He* drove it into the tree,' said Barbara.

'I was distracted.'

'Still your fault.'

'You turned the wipers on.'

'It was raining.'

'No, it wasn't.'

'You had an accident in 1973?' asked Scarlett.

'No seatbelts; thrown through the windscreen; horrible mess,' said Barbara. 'It hurt. A lot.' She grabbed her left shoulder and pulled it away from her body revealing a hideous, gruesome wound that severed her arm and sliced her body almost in two.

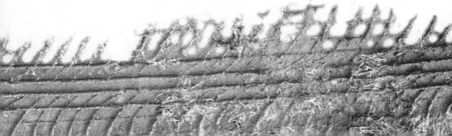

'Bar! Don't!' Brian protested. 'She's showing off.' He smiled at Scarlett again.

Scar's ghost-heart beat faster. She couldn't believe that she hadn't worked it out sooner. What an idiot! After wasting all that time trying to kill her friends, she'd had a couple of ready-made ghost-friends right here, in the park. Maybe even a ghost-*boyfriend*.

'You can show her yours,' said Barbara, pushing the top of her arm bone back into the shoulder socket.

'She doesn't want to see my injuries,' said Brian, blushing as much as a ghost can blush.

'It's OK,' said Scarlett. 'You can show me if you like.' She was actually ghoulishly fascinated and couldn't wait to see how he'd died.

Brian shrugged and his head fell off. Then, holding his head in one hand, he pressed his chest with the other and his ribs collapsed, revealing a gory basin in his torso, like the inside of a scooped-out grapefruit.

'You're dead!' Scarlett grinned. 'That's fantastic!'

ADVICE FOR THE NEWLY-DEAD TEENAGER.

So you're dead? Here's what to do...

Step One – Take a deep breath. I know this sounds really dumb because, basically, you don't breathe anymore, but, I promise you, it'll make you feel a whole lot better.

Step Two – Don't panic about how weird everything feels. I know! Freaky, isn't it? You'll begin to get the hang of sinking and floating in no time. Or S'n'F, as I call it. I've devised a really great yoga-based workout that gets all the right S'n'F muscles tuned up. Just click on the link.

Step Three – TRUST NO ONE – apart from me, Scarlett, obviously! There are spooks and ghouls out there, especially online, who'll give you really BAD advice. Stick with me and I'll get you through this as painlessly as possible. I promise.

The
Dedd
End.

Visit Scar's Blog at http://scardeparted.blogspot.com

She's totally reformed and promises she won't try to kill you!

 But she will give you the latest goss on
her blossoming romance with ghost-boy Brian…

And she's negotiating with her not-yet-dead friends to let
her post some clips from the gore-fest, bloodbath horror
films they made together like *Zombie Saturday Checkout
Girl* and *Cuddly Bunny Meets the Hair Salon Slasher*…you
know you want to see those!

About the Author

Cathy Brett

has been scribbling stuff for more than twenty years,
as a fashion illustrator; as a jet-setting spotter of
global trends and as a consultant to the
behemoths of the British high street.

She now lectures in design and unashamedly
plunders her students' lives for sensational
storylines and characters.